Must Love Spankings

Tina Sumley

Splurge Publishing

MUST
LOVE
SPANKINGS

Tina Sumley

Splurge Publishing

Published by Splurge Publishing, Spring Hill, TN 37174

Printed in the United States of America.

CONTENTS

1. Questionable Behavior 1

2. Red Velvet 9

3. Know Him A Little Bit 17

4. Image 29

5. Fitzwilliam Darcy 43

6. Company Handbook............... 57

7. New Rules 65

8. For What It's Worth 93

9. Complete Acceptance........... 109

10. The Past Is Never Far 127

11. To The Ground..................... 143

12. Chaos Of The Hurricane 165

13. If Only 181

14. Dumping Mr. Darcy 201

15. Running On Empty............. 211

16. Hideaway 225

17. Glimmer 239

18. The Wait Of It All 259

Chapter 1
QUESTIONABLE BEHAVIOR

If Hell were a bar, it would be one too small to be considered intimate, too grimy to be considered a hole in the wall, and too hot for the ceiling fan to do anything but sound like it's about to break.

The man sitting slumped over on the stool beside me isn't very attractive, but I've drunk enough that I care a lot less about his face than the fact that his hand is on my knee and he looks strong enough to break me in two.

"We get a bad rap as these junk-eating, crude jerks that hog the road, but I'm okay with that reputation. I mean, I get to see all of America. Well, most of America. Obviously, I can't get to Hawaii and I've never been to Alaska."

I twirl my hair around my finger; the strands pulled so tight that I can feel the tip of my finger go numb. I let go, leaning toward him.

"It must be pretty lonely driving around all of the time."

He tucks the strand of hair behind my ear, but it falls back in front of my face. He doesn't try to fix it again. "You know, if you're really interested in big rigs, I could give you a ride."

I like this tension between us and the fact that I know he's already imagined me under him and himself ramming into me. It's like being the matador in a bullfight – the danger and pain are almost as thrilling as the conquest.

"I'm sure you could." I bite my lower lip, trying to concentrate enough to make a decision. Most people who know me don't know that I'm a champion of questionable behavior – trying unknown drugs, getting drunk enough to blackout, hanging out with people who are known and despised by the NYPD – but I'm usually too cautious about pregnancy or STDs to actually sleep with a stranger.

Still, a man taking control is enough to make my heart beat faster and want to give him all of my control.

Big Rig raps his fingers against the bar. 'Come on. I bought you a couple shots. That's enough for you to polish my chrome."

I don't feel like giving this man my control. It's been fun flirting, but there's no ache between my legs and no rush to do anything to his chrome. His confidence comes off more as insecurity blanketed by bravado. One little push could send him into hysterics and I'm not interested in being a babysitter.

"You know what?" I say. "I actually have to get up early in the morning. I'm starting a new job."

His eyes narrow. "Our arrangement shouldn't take

more than five minutes."

I glance over toward the right corner of the bar, where Erin is playing darts with a couple of men. She has the worst eyesight God has ever given anyone, but with the help of glasses, she can hustle even the best dart players. She already has a fat wad of cash in her back pocket.

She's also not paying me any attention.

"That doesn't sound like something to brag about," I say back to Big Rig. I turn, taking a couple of steps toward the dartboard. He grabs my arm, jerking me around so hard that I would have fallen on my face if his grip wasn't so tight.

"You don't get to be a tease like that without giving something in return." He yanks me toward him. I fall against his chest. For the first time in recent memory, danger feels like something I should be fleeing instead of pursuing.

"Hey!"

As I hear Erin's voice, Big Rig lets me go. I fall onto my ass, the cement sending a shock of pain through my body. I quickly scramble onto my feet. I smell Erin's floral perfume as she steps up behind me.

"Why don't you get going, buddy?" she asks. "If she doesn't want to tango, she doesn't want to tango."

He glances between the two of us before sneering. "Who are you? Her savior? Her warrior princess?"

"I don't come from the Amazon, but I am from a

state that believes in shooting first and asking questions later."

His sneer fades and he takes a step back. He sends me one last withering look.

"It would have been a pity fuck anyway," he says. He turns around and stomps to the door. He slams it so hard that there are a few seconds of awkward silence in the bar until everyone decides to pretend it never happened.

I stumble back to the bar. As I pay for a Lsong Island iced tea, Erin sits down beside me where Big Rig had just been. Her golden hair is twisted into a braid and she's wearing a large plaid shirt over jeans, but she's still the hottest person in the bar.

"Why don't I take you home now?" she suggests, as I stir the drink with my straw. "I've beaten all of these guys. None of them will face me again, so I can't earn anything else."

"That's not the real reason you want to take me home," I say.

"You're right. I want to make sure that guy isn't waiting in the parking lot to kill you."

"I'm not a little kid, Erin."

"No, you're a reckless adult."

I sip from the straw. "I can get a cab. You can leave whenever you want. I'm really fine."

She shakes her head, muttering something about responsibility.

I lean against the bar, sipping from my glass. The last thing I remember is Erin's hand on my shoulder, asking me if I'm ready to go now.

*****

My eyelids feel like anchors. My body feels like there are bruises where my muscles should be. In general, I feel like shit, but there's a loud clanking that won't stop, so I open my eyes.

Erin's blurry figure walks up to me. As she becomes clearer, I see she's carrying a large glass of green sludge. She hands it to me and I look down into the glass. The shade of green reminds me of algae. The sludge is just as lumpy too.

"Did this come from under my sink?" I ask.

"It's an old recipe from my grandpa. He used to work in a factory Monday through Friday and he'd get drunk on Friday, but he had to get up early on Saturdays to work at his parent's farm. He didn't want to give up his drinking, so he spent years perfecting this recipe. It should dull your headache."

"They have invented aspirin you know. And I don't have a headache."

"Liar."

I take a sip from the green sludge. At first, it's almost good – tastes a bit like spinach, a little gritty, and it could use some sugar – but the aftertaste hits me and I realize hangovers aren't the worst thing in the world.

"You know, if you never find the perfect man, that's fine," Erin says. "It's not like men are necessary to...please yourself."

"Yeah, I've tried that. It doesn't work," I say. "You have a boyfriend. You know how different it is to have an actual man – warm skin, rough hands, the surprises, his mouth on you...his…"

She smirks. I'm sure she's being swept away by a memory of the last time Tom had been home from his office in France. He might be a bit plain, but he's madly in love with her and I suppose it makes all the difference in her case.

"I'm just worried," she says. "But I figured you would say that, so while you were sleeping I decided on a safer route for you."

"Please tell me it's not online dating."

"It's online dating!"

I groan. "Erin."

"Sarah, listen, this site I found for you is amazing. It uses these psychology methods along with your interests, your views of the world, and how you like to spend your free time to pair you with the best men. I didn't do any of the tests yet, but I had it set up with your photo, that you're twenty-four and added a description that talked about how you had a good paying job–"

"I have an internship that I haven't started yet. How is that–"

"Sarah, once they see your profile picture, most won't care about what your job is. I chose that one from the park when you were wearing that red blouse that contrasted well with your dark hair and made you look, um, curvier than you are."

"You are getting excellent at the backhanded compliments."

"You realize that was *still* a compliment though, right?"

"No. It was sarcasm."

"Well, the site sent you an email to verify your account. I wrote your password on a sticky note left by your laptop. If you love me, you'll try at least a few dates."

"You're assuming someone will be interested in me."

Her eyes focus on the glass of green sludge. I bring it up to my lips, pretending to take a drink. I shouldn't be such a jerk to her. She's the oldest of six siblings. This is how she expresses her love: overbearing, overthought, and overdone.

"Thank you, Erin. I promise I'll go on at least two dates."

"Three."

"Two," I repeat. "Two is enough."

"Fine. I have to get to work. You have to get ready too. It takes half an hour to get to the Torv Global building if there's heavy traffic, which there will be and it's almost 7 o'clock."

I shake my head. "You're like the mom I never wanted–"

Her smile falters.

"–but needed," I finish. I stand up and give her a hug. She hugs me back tighter and then points to the green sludge.

"Finish that or regret it."

Chapter 2
RED VELVET

I regret not finishing the green sludge.

The whole building is celebrating the retirement of a woman named Marge. I know nobody here, the noise is slicing through my brain, my head feels like it's two sizes too large and all I want to do is sleep. It doesn't help that at least a dozen people have told me their name and I can't remember any of them except that I'm pretty sure there's two men named Chris. But I'm only pretty sure because I may have just introduced myself to the same man twice.

Torv Global is a Fortune 500 company that originally only dealt with fitness equipment but has expanded to various other fields. I would have expected a company like this to offer only limp broccoli with fat-free ranch dressing, so I'm surprised when red velvet cake is offered. I'm even more surprised that it tastes like holiness and sinfulness at the same time.

"Mr. Garrett would never give anyone else a retirement party if they quit at the last minute like this."

With the plastic fork still in my mouth, I look

around the corner. There's a short woman in a flower pattern dress drinking from a plastic cup standing next to a man around my age with glasses that are too small for his face. The man nibbles on his slice of cake.

"She was like his mother though," the man says, his voice lower pitched than I imagined. "I heard that her husband is sick or something. She needed to leave."

The woman glances up at the man. I pretend to be focusing on slathering the icing onto the side of my cake.

"So, who's going to be Mr. Garrett's assistant now?" the woman asks. "It'd be a pay bump for me. The company has to be accepting resumes already, right?"

"I dunno," the man says. "I wouldn't do it. I hate unpredictable jobs and—"

He stops. Nearly everyone stops—stops moving, stops talking, even their eyes seem to freeze on something to my right. I turn, my motion feeling disruptive in the stillness.

I take a step back. If power corrupts, then I'm completely corrupted because the man who walked through the door is radiating power, charisma, and warmth like a fire. His dirty blond hair looks slightly windswept to the right, but it doesn't look messy—more like a devil-may-care attitude. His jawline is chiseled enough that I'm fairly certain if someone punched his face, their fingers would snap.

"Michael, you need to tell John that we need his

proposal by tomorrow," this man says. "If he can't come up with anything, he's gone."

"Absolutely, Mr. Garrett," a shorter man beside him says. "I was going to say the exact same thing, but I wanted to make sure it's what you wanted."

"Mr. Garrett," a redhead steps up to him. "The advertisement for the new energy drink is going amazing, but we have an issue. Maggie Reynolds was arrested for a DWI, so we need a new model."

"Thank you, Chelsea. Call Kate Andrés. If she's not available, try Amber Palmer. How's your father doing?"

"Oh, he's doing great. The chemotherapy seems to be working," the redhead says. He nods.

"I'm glad. If you need anything, just tell me."

He turns to the man next to her.

"Rafael, how's Camila?"

"She's doing great, Mr. Garrett. She still uses that stuffed unicorn you bought her as a pillow."

"She's almost a year old now, isn't she?"

"Yes. It's hard to believe."

"Tell your Hannah I said 'hello.' Will you?"

"I will, sir. Thank you."

Rafael backs away and lowers his head as though his moment with the king is over. Mr. Garrett's eyes sweep around the room, landing on me. I'm staring like an idiot, so I drop my gaze from his face. But it doesn't help as I focus on his clearly tailor-made suit and what is, I'm certain, a body that was only made possible by a personal trainer and unrelenting self-discipline.

"Hi, I'm Finn." He extends his hand. I reach to shake his hand, my fingers clumsily getting in the way before he manages to grasp it. It's a firm grip, but not tight enough for me to think he's trying to prove anything.

"Yes. Hi."

At the last second, I remember to smile, so I only look half as hopeless as I feel.

"And you are?"

"Oh, right." I turn my face, hoping he doesn't see that I'm blushing. "I'm Sarah. Sarah Moore."

He nods, but he doesn't look away from me like normal social relations would require. His eyes are a piercing blue that makes me feel like he has stripped me of clothes, pretenses, and everything around us, and he knows there was never a doubt that he is the guest of honor to everything in my soul.

Then, he walks away.

*****

My arms reach around Finn's waist. The motorcycle is thunderous as it speeds down an endless highway. I lean against his back, feeling his body heat against me, and the rumble of the motor between my legs.

He slows down at a red light. We're alone on the

road. It's not raining, but the city is glistening in a way that I've only seen in old movies.

Finn hits the kickstand with his heel and gets off the bike. As his hands move to pull off my helmet, I can almost imagine those hands on my face, on my waist, between my thighs. He pulls off my helmet and drops it. I can smell the rain coating the city mixed with his woodsy, masculine scent now and the scent gets stronger as he leans forward, his lips slightly parted. I close my eyes and lean forward too—

Then, sirens.

I jerk awake, my lips still puckered. It's not a siren. It's my alarm clock. I run my fingers over my lips, trying to hide my embarrassment over something so simple when no one else can even see me. Clearly, it's been too long since I've been in bed with a man.

Sure, Finn is attractive, charismatic, rich, and seems like a genuinely good guy who remembered everyone's names and cared about the details of their lives, but there are plenty of other guys like that. Or maybe not plenty, but surely a dozen or so. Maybe.

I turn off my phone's alarm, lie back down and close my eyes. I try to cement the dream in my memory. Everything about it felt real, even the rumble of the motor and the heat of Finn's body.

I check emails on my phone. I blink several times. Usually, I only have a dozen or so new emails with most of it going straight to the spam folder, but there's nearly double that now and eight of them have a subject line that starts with "You have a new message on Letters of Love."

The online dating site that Erin signed me up for. I had thoughtlessly verified my account and forgotten about it since I saw Finn, but I promised Erin I'd try it.

I click on the first email.

Hey what's up?

I delete the message. I move on to the second email.

Hello! My name is Jason. I am a stand-up comedian. A lot of people think I'm just a dreamer, but I actually made an appearance in a movie called Big Shots (I was the one doing a keg stand). I don't have a lot of money right now, but we all believe in equality, so women have a lot of dates to make up to men, right? Haha! Hope to hear from you soon!!!

Delete.

Are you an angel? Because you look like you just fell from Heaven.

Delete.

Sorry messed that line up. It's supposed to be Did it hurt when you fell from heaven? Oh well. You got more pics?

Delete.

My cocks name is Godzilla and it wants to destroy your Tokyo.

Delete. That comedian is looking pretty good right

about now.

Hi, Sarah. My name is Hank. I don't know how to do these things, so I guess I'll just tell you about myself. I'm 26 (almost 27). I'm going to school to be a pediatrician. I love hiking and reading. I'm pretty much interested in anything you're willing to get into—a hook-up, relationship, just friends, etc.. I just feel like I don't have much time to date, so I thought I'd try this out. If you're not interested, that's cool too. I get it. It must be scary to meet men over the internet.

I click on a link that leads to his profile. He's cute—thin-rimmed glasses, short brown hair, a little skinny for my taste, but he looks perfectly normal and normal seems to be the gold standard on this website.

I check the other emails. They're all similar to the first few I read. I send a quick reply to Hank, and then set my phone down.

It will be another couple days before I go back to *Torv Global*. I've researched into Finn—he's the CEO, so in all likelihood, he's rarely there, and so far out of my league, I might as well daydream about Leonardo DiCaprio. I close my eyes. I see Finn on that bike again and smile.

Chapter 3
KNOW HIM A LITTLE BIT

I hand my mother her glasses as we stand in her kitchen. Everything in this room feels like it's older than I am—there's even that avocado green refrigerator from the 1970s.

"You texted me about your dates, but you never told me how they went," she mutters as she fills the tin kettle with water and sets it on the stove. She turns the knob and I watch the flames reach up toward the kettle. That damn kettle gets more heat and human contact than I do.

"Well, on Saturday night, I went out with Hank," I say.

"The pediatrician."

"Yep. He was nice. We saw a movie and had dinner. But I don't know. He asked me if he could kiss me. I said yes. He kissed me. I didn't feel anything. The whole date felt a little strange—like we were in middle school or something—but he was a nice guy. Nice."

"But you want something more."

"I don't know if I want more after my second date.

His name was Josh and it all started very normal, but he just kept talking about his job. For the whole date. Maybe he was just nervous. But then he got drunk during dinner and just complained on and on about his co-workers."

"So, you weren't attracted to either of these men?"

"Not really, no."

"Have you felt anything for anyone recently?"

I watch my mother take out a mug from her corner cabinet.

"Well, no one I really know."

My mother raises her eyebrow, setting the mug on the counter. "No one you really know? That means you must know him a little bit. That's a start. You just have to get out of your own way, lady."

I chew on the inside of my cheek. The last thing I want to admit is that my mother is right, but I've only had a couple of relationships and I wasn't in love with either of them. I've never been willing to completely let go and step into a relationship without reservations.

The kettle starts to whistle. My mother pours the water into her mug and adds the teabag. She lets it brew until it's perfect.

*****

"So, when you answer the phone, you say Hello, this is Sarah at Torv Global. How may I assist you?

Nothing more, nothing less. The extension numbers are taped right here. If there is something that you're not sure how to respond to, you tell them you need to confer with your manager." My manager, Gwen, points to herself like I could have forgotten who she is. "You never tell anyone that you can't do something for them. All of the people who call this number are important— or, at least, we treat them like they're important. If they ask you for a giraffe, you tell them that you will call them back because you need to call all of the zoos in the state. Then, we will find another way to make them happy. Got it?"

"Got it," I say.

"Follow me."

I follow her down a hallway. We both jolt to a stop as a door swings open and a group of men step out, a couple of them speed walking from the back to be next to the leader of the pack.

My heart feels like the bike's motor in my dream as I see the one in front is Finn. As Gwenn and I follow behind him, I can smell that he actually does have a woodsy scent. My subconscious must have remembered it from when we met, tucking it away for my dream. I'm also becoming immensely aware of why everything was wet in that dream.

Gwenn's eyes trace Finn's body for the briefest second. I feel jealousy slice through me. The only way I can think to calm myself is to focus on something.

My mind decides to focus on Finn's hands.

His hands move as he explains something to one of the men walking beside him. For a split second, I think he glances back at me, but he continues talking without missing a beat. He shows the man beside him a sticky note. As he places it back on the folder he's carrying, it doesn't quite stick and his hand brushes against the folder. I watch the note flutter in the air between us like a yellow petal.

I stoop to pick it up. It has somebody's phone number on it.

"Ah, Mr. Garrett, sir?"

He turns. "Yes, Ms. Moore?"

"You dropped this."

I hold out the note to him. As he takes it, I feel his fingertips brush against my skin. They're rougher than I expect and it sends a wave of heat through my body.

He takes the note as his eyes linger on mine and in a display of self-discipline, he abstains from snooping through every damn square inch of my soul as he could easily have done. "Thank you," he says. "It's nice that someone is attentive."

As he walks away, the man beside him says, "Sir, I think I'm attentive."

Gwenn and I turn to the copy machines. As Gwenn is about to speak, I hear Finn call out.

"Ms. Moore."

I turn toward him as though the General of the

Army yelled my name, my skin feeling strangely cold and deprived of human contact.

"I'd like for you to be in my office at 2:00 today. I'd like to speak with you about a position."

I incline my head slightly in what I hope looks like a nod. My whole body doesn't seem to want to work for me anymore—it just wants to slide down onto the floor and transform into a single needy nerve.

He gives me a small smile. I turn away so he can't see me blush, my fingers combing through my dark brown hair, hoping it doesn't look like as much of a mess as I feel.

As Gwenn explains to me the procedure of using the copy machine, I remain painfully aware of where Finn is, the way his body moves, and the way his eyes glance over at me every few minutes. I shake my head at the near over-the-top thought that announces itself in my mind. For the first time in my life, I have met someone who makes me feel completely naked – both physically and emotionally. When he looks at me I feel open, vulnerable, and exposed. His eyes know me.

*****

1:57.

I stare at the phone, willing it to ring, so I can have an excuse to delay my meeting with Finn.

I wait.

And wait.

Waiting.

1:58.

I can't be late to a meeting with the CEO of the company where I'm interning. I stand up. I imagine myself as Cinderella, recently transformed from a lowly servant girl into a beautiful woman with a flowing gown and simple, gorgeous jewelry. When the handsome prince sees me, all he'll see is a woman who knows what she's doing.

There's a thick kidney-shaped mahogany desk outside of Finn's office. A thin older woman with short gray hair is sitting behind it, typing on a sleek laptop. It's Marge—his assistant who was having the retirement party on my first day here. I remember seeing her, but I never had the chance to introduce myself.

"That's a beautiful desk," I blurt out. She glances up at me and smiles.

"Yes, it was a gift from Mr. Garrett," she says. "It doesn't quite fit in with the modern style of everything else, but when we chose the new furniture, Mr. Garrett noticed my preference for the more rustic look, so he made an exception for me."

"That's incredibly nice of him," I say. "He seems like a great boss."

"Yes he is. I'm sad to be leaving, but it's time. My husband needs me. Let me tell you, Miss…"

"Sarah," I say. "Sarah Moore."

"Miss Moore. Time goes very quickly in life. For someone as young as you, it might seem slow, but it just keeps getting quicker. Find what you love—a person, a job, a place—and keep hold of it. Never lose sight of any of it."

"Thank you," I say, though the advice seems like it only works for those with enough money to not be working every second, enough money to chase after their dream job, and enough money to go to the place they want to live. "I'm sorry, I have a meeting with Mr. Garrett."

"Oh, of course, I'm sorry. Go right in. I'm sure he's waiting for you."

I knock on the door.

"Come in."

The nervous pulse through my stomach actually helps me push the door open.

I'm not sure what I expected. Most of the office is stainless steel, everything as sleek as I'd expect a Fortune 500 company to look. But Finn's office goes beyond sleek. Everything makes me think of the blade of a sword—sharp edges and reflective. On the left, there's a black leather couch and recliner with a glass coffee table between it. A few feet from there, there's a long black marble table with six leather chairs surrounding it. The wall across from me isn't a wall— it's just one long window and I can see the city sprawled out in front of me. To my right, is an L-shaped marble desk with Finn sitting behind it.

"Are you going to come over for our meeting?" he asks. I flush and hustle over from the door before it occurs to me that he's only teasing me. Still, I fumble to sit in the leather chair across from him, then struggle to lower the chair so that my feet aren't dangling. When I finally look at him—avoiding the penetrating soul-gaze of his beautiful blue eyes—his eyebrow is slightly raised and there's a hint of a smile on his face. "Comfortable?"

"Yeah. Yes sir," I say, a bit breathless after everything. He presses his index finger near his temple before letting it trail down his face. I imagine the feeling of his 5 o'clock shadow and the warmth of his skin. I take a deep breath, trying to refocus by looking behind him. Mind over matter. "I'm good. Thank you."

"Do you know why I asked you in here?"

There are several trophies behind him, many of them with a gold or glass golf ball incorporated into it. That would explain his tan that makes his blue eyes so much more prominent.

"You said you wanted to talk to me about a position."

His smile deepens the slightest bit. "Yes."

"I haven't been here long at all, but if you think I'd be better suited for another position, I'd be glad to do it. Do the job, I mean. Not that it could mean anything else. What I mean is—"

"You can take a breath, Sarah," he says. "It's

okay. Just pretend we're having a casual conversation in a break room."

"Okay, sure," I say like I'm perfectly capable of doing what he said.

"This is about the assistant job," he says. "You would be working directly under me. Is that fine?"

I swallow. Directly under him. "Yes. Of course."

"So, tell me, why did you choose to intern here?"

The brother of Erin's boyfriend used to work here. She suggested it. There's nothing deeper or more meaningful, but I know he wants a better answer than that.

"Um. Well…I love…fitness," I say. I look down at my hands. It's so hard to concentrate when his face is…existing in front of me. "I mean, your clothing line, your dumbbells, the…everything. Everything is great that you guys do."

"What do you like to do for fitness?"

"Run." It's what I'd like to do right now before I look like an even bigger fool.

"Are you good at memorizing a lot of information?"

"Definitely." Or, at least, possibly.

"How are your computer skills?"

"Great," I say. "I know how to use word processors, email, and all of those kinds of things."

The only skill I could add to that list is knowing how to use a search engine to figure out how to do everything else.

"Are you discreet?"

"Yes."

"Is your schedule flexible? If someone needed you at 9 o'clock on a Friday night, would you be able to assist them?"

"Yes," I say. One-word answers seem to be the key here. He doesn't seem interested in doubting me.

"If there was an issue, would you be able to solve it without needing to ask anyone for help?"

I blink. "It depends on the issue. That's kind of obvious, isn't it? If the building was on fire, I wouldn't try to create a whole new sprinkler system. I'd call the fire department."

There's a pause. I look up. His face is unreadable, but he leans back into his chair.

"Thank you, Miss Moore. That will conclude this interview."

Heat rises up to my face. I should have kept doing the one-word answers. I'm going to lose my internship over my obsession with technicalities.

I stand up, thrusting my hand forward. "Thank you for the interview, sir."

He stands up and shakes my hand. "It was my pleasure."

I spin around, trying to look as confident as possible as I stride toward the door. I'm such an idiot. I won't let myself be so distracted by a man's appearance, personality, charisma, and everything about him ever again.

"Miss Moore."

I hesitate at the door. I turn to look at him. Even from this distance, his eyes glow like blue flames.

"You'll start tomorrow."

"Really?"

"Really."

"Thank you so much, Mr. Garrett."

He nods. "You're welcome."

I open the door.

"Miss Moore?"

I turn.

"I suggest you bring a fire extinguisher. Just in case of a fire in the building."

I frown, thinking of all the fire extinguishers I've seen in the building. He smiles and the faintest laugh escapes from his lips.

"I'm kidding, Miss Moore."

"Of course, right, I know," I say, smiling back like an idiot. I slip out the door as quickly as I can, nearly running back toward the phone. I slide back into my chair, closing my eyes. I replay his handshake, his laugh, and the way he leaned back with his hands clasped near his groin.

My heart starts beating faster. I open my eyes, taking a deep breath and trying to focus on working again. I slide on my reading glasses and try to focus on the documents in front of me. Then, it feels like my lungs drop down to my feet.

I'm going to be Finn Garrett's assistant. I'm going to have to be around him all the time without falling apart or turning into a desperate school girl.

I cover my face with my hands. I truly may need a fire extinguisher and an astonishing amount of help.

Chapter 4
IMAGE

Kate Andrés, the new model for Torv Vitality energy drink is standing in front of me, her fingers tapping on the mahogany desk while I'm on the phone with a very angry Frenchman.

"I'm sorry, Mr. Faure. Mr. Garrett consulted with several financial advisors and they all agreed that the advertisement for the new French fitness clothing line would—"

"I do not care what any financial advisor said. My people can do a lot with that $5,000 that you are cutting from the budget—"

"Mr. Faure, it's just being reinvested into the advertisements. You know Mr. Garrett wouldn't make this decision without being certain it would work for the best—"

"Ma'am," Kate says. "I need to speak to Mr. Garrett now."

"I'm sorry," I say, half to Jack Faure and half to Kate. Apologizing feels like half my job. "Mr. Faure, Mr. Garrett told me he would call you later tonight and explain everything to you."

"I do not want to hear from him unless he gives me back the original budget we discussed."

"I'm sorry," I say. "I'm sure both of you will find a way to work this out."

Kate snatches the phone out of my hand.

"Mr. Faure, it's Kate Andrés," she purrs. "How are you? I'm wonderful. Do you remember the last time Mr. Garrett cut your budget? That's right. You don't remember because it has never happened. I have my full faith in Mr. Garrett, don't you? Yes, that's what I thought. Okay. Okay. I will see you soon, I'm sure."

She sets the phone down beside my hand and crosses her arms over her chest.

"I need to talk to Mr. Garrett immediately," she says.

"I heard you before," I say, tucking my hair behind my ear. "But I'm sorry. Mr. Garrett is in a meeting right now."

I thought being Finn's assistant would mean the hardest part of my job would be working so close to him, but I've found that he does a thousand things a day and I'm just around to pick up the other hundred things he doesn't have time for.

"Ma'am, you don't understand. I'm Kate Andrés. He will want to see me. Tell him I'm here. Now, please."

I didn't like this woman on sight. She's thinner

than I could ever dream to be, has to be nearly six feet tall, making me look even shorter than I already am, and she's dressed like she stepped out of a bohemian-style magazine, bare midriff included. Now, she's talking like she and Finn are close to each other. I'm not usually a jealous type, but it feels so incredibly cliché for a handsome millionaire to slip into bed with a foreign diva model.

"I will tell him as soon as his meeting is over," I say.

She mutters something in a language I don't understand, but I get the general idea that it wasn't a compliment.

I type up an email that Finn needed me to write for a website designer about the company website. As I click send, Finn's door opens.

George Yang steps out first, followed by Finn.

"Thank you, George," Finn says. "Your stories are always entertaining. Make sure to tell your wife that I can't wait to have her shrimp wontons again."

"She'll be happy to hear that," George says. He gives Kate and me a small nod as he passes. Kate gives a dramatic sigh that sounds a lot like a dying bird and wraps her arms around Finn's neck, kissing his left cheek.

"Finn, lovely, I've been calling your phone all day. Are you playing hard to get?"

He carefully takes her arm and unwraps it from

his neck. "Kate, what are you doing here?"

"I thought we could have lunch or drinks or something. I miss you."

For the briefest second, he glances over at me. Or maybe his eye just caught my movement as I pretended to type up a new email. He puts his hand on her mid back and guides her a few feet into his office but not out of my line of sight. He begins speaking to her in a hushed voice that I'm not sure he wanted to completely prevent me from hearing. "Nothing happened between us, Kate. I only took you to that fundraiser because I needed a date and we had just met the week before. I thought you understood that."

Kate takes a step back. "Oh. Well, that doesn't mean we can't try something now. There's this great little restaurant around the corner that makes amazing salads. I mean, I've heard they make great burgers too. I haven't tried them yet, but we could try them together."

"I'm sorry. I'm very busy." He walks out of his office and turns to me. "The meeting with Jack Foley is in a half hour, correct?"

"Yes," I say.

"You should take your lunch break. How are you feeling so far about the job?"

Overwhelmed. Unprepared. Embarrassed over my own inadequacy.

"Great," I say.

His mouth curls up in a slight smirk as though he's

not buying my answer. Kate taps his shoulder. He turns toward her with a slight annoyance on his face.

"I just…thank you for the opportunity to work on the ad."

"You're welcome, Miss Andrés."

Her thinness and bohemian-style suddenly make me think of a young child as she bites her lip, taking an uncertain step back. She spins around, her long skirt swaying around her as she heads toward the elevators. Finn watches her leave for a few seconds before turning back toward me.

"I hope that wasn't awkward for you. I just wanted her to know exactly where we stood."

"No, it was fine," I say. "I'm sure you meet a lot of models in your work and take them to a lot of…fundraisers."

"Part of the reason we are successful as a company is because of our image. The board of directors likes the more high-profile employees to stay fit and keep a beautiful woman on their arm."

"What about the female high-profile employees?"

He shrugs. "Most of them are married."

He takes a pen out of the cup on my desk, pulls out the top drawer and takes out a pad of sticky notes. He jots something down, and then hands it to me. It's a phone number.

"This is my private cell number if you need to get ahold of me quickly."

"I already have your work cell phone number."

"I know. But I don't answer my work number when I'm eating or else I'd never have time to eat."

My finger smudges the last number on the sticky note as I read it.

"This is the same number from the sticky note that you dropped before," I say. "I mean, the one that slipped that I picked up."

"Like I said, you're attentive. I only gave Daniel my number because he kept calling Marge to touch base with me and Marge didn't appreciate being called at midnight."

"You don't mind being called at midnight?"

"Only by the people who have that number. I trust them to only call when absolutely necessary and to be extremely protective of my information." He stands up straighter, sliding a hand into a pocket. "You should get some lunch. There's a bistro on the first floor that makes a variety of food, but if you want my personal recommendation, there's also a mom and pop pizzeria a few blocks north that makes amazing pizza margherita."

"Thanks, I might just do that."

He hesitates at my desk. This is the first time I've seen him that he doesn't seem to be completely in control of a situation. I'm fairly certain there's a company policy against us being together—but the moment is surreal as I consider the notion that he *could* be interested in me.

"I want you to be comfortable in this new position," he says. "With Marge's husband being sick, I let some things be pushed back, so she didn't feel pressured to keep up. But I can't let the company suffer because of my choices. It could affect other people's jobs and lives."

"Of course," I say. I cup my chin in my hand, trying to hide my embarrassment. He wasn't interested in me at all. He was just treating me with kid gloves because he's still not sure I can do this job. "But I'm fine. I can handle it. You're right, though, I should get some lunch. Excuse me."

I grab my bag, jerking so fast out of my chair that my shoulder hits against his shoulder. I don't look back as I rush to the elevators. I click the down arrow several times, but it can't come fast enough.

*****

"How's the job?" Erin asks, swirling her glass of wine before taking a sip. In my apartment's kitchen, she seems strangely tall, which just reminds me of Kate Andrés. I take a gulp of my own wine, barely tasting it before it joins the amazing pizza margherita slice I had this afternoon.

"Do you remember that time I worked as a rodeo clown?"

"You never worked as a rodeo clown."

"Well, I feel like I have now. I can consider myself an experienced rodeo clown after this job. I have to contact all these quick-tempered people and be as entertaining as possible to avoid being trampled to death by all of them."

"Come on. It can't be that bad. At least it pays well, right?"

"Yeah, and Finn is nice enough not to call me late at night. Remember how Beth used to get called all the time when she was an assistant to that chef, who wanted to make his own TV show?"

Erin nods. "I remember her running out during her sister's baby shower because he desperately needed her to stand in line to get some video game that was coming out nine hours later."

We both take long sips of our wine. Neither of us have heard from Beth in a while, but it's because of a more demanding boss than Chef Bennet—her four month old baby.

"The pay is great," I say. "The people are just…very challenging."

"What about your boss? He must not be that bad if you're referring to him on a first name basis. I've read up on him. He's taken quite a few model types to events, but as far as I can tell, he's remained on the city's most eligible bachelor's list."

"So?"

She shrugs. "I was just curious if he acts like an

eligible bachelor."

"He cares about his work. That's it. That's all. There's absolutely nothing else he cares about. He's a complete gentleman." I sigh.

"That was a very aggressive proclamation."

"Well, you're always on my ass about dating. I'm not so desperate to risk my job by throwing myself at my boss."

"All I did was ask about him."

"And tried to get me to find a boyfriend through online dating."

"And you only went on two dates."

"I told you I'd only go on two dates. I kept my promise."

"So, you're just giving up?"

"I'm taking a break," I say. "I just started a new job I suck at. I'd like to suck at one thing at a time."

"Sarah."

"Erin."

She sets her empty wine glass down. "Did you even look at any of the other profiles?"

"No, and I unsubscribed from getting emails from the site because I just kept getting strange messages from weird men."

"You should look at some profiles," she says. "You can search for specific types."

She walks over to my laptop and hands it to me. "Just look around on the site. You still need to get laid."

"How do you know that I didn't sleep with one of my dates and just didn't tell you about it? I could've had crazy hot sex and left my panties at one of their apartments and just didn't tell you."

She looks me up and down. "If you'd had sex recently, I'd be able to tell. If your body was any tenser, you'd be in rigor mortis."

I glare at her, but she just grabs her purse and gives me a hug.

"We'll talk later. Tom is coming back tomorrow, so we'll be, uh, very busy for the next couple days."

"I guess I won't hear from you for a few days then," I say. "Try to come up for air once in a while."

"No promises."

I watch her step out of my apartment. I open up my laptop and go to the *Letters of Love* website. I ignore the 10 messages waiting for me and click *Find Love*.

PREFERRED AGE GROUP [check all that apply]:

I select 20-30 and 30-40. There's an option that says, "Add 5 Years" and I click it as well.

PREFERRED LOCATION:

Within 25 miles.

WHAT KIND OF RELATIONSHIP ARE YOU LOOKING FOR?:

Any of the above.

I hesitate on the last two: preferred body type and preferred height. I'd like to imagine I'm not especially shallow, but to pretend I don't have a preference feels like a pretentious lie. I select Athletic for body type and 5'9" or taller for height.

I have 44 matches.

I suppress a groan. I just have to choose one person who is not a psychopath to show Erin that I tried to find a boyfriend. After this, she's going to owe me at least one dinner and possibly a kitten, so I can start my descent into becoming an old cat lady.

First profile: *My name's Kyle. I love hockey, rock music, old cars, and afternoon delights if you know what I mean. If you don't know what I mean, I mean lunchtime sex.*

I'm tempted to send a message, asking him if he loves those things in that order, but I decide to pass over the profile. I can already imagine a scenario where Kyle is explaining every sexual innuendo as we're having sex.

I slowly look through each profile. Two of them look promising—while one is a bit too gothic for my taste and the other wouldn't quite be considered to have an athletic body, but at least he doesn't seem insane.

Then I see the most beautiful dog that has ever graced the planet.

The Siberian Husky seems to be striding down a beach, its pale blue eyes glowing in the dusk. The name of the profile is Fitzwilliam Darcy. From *Pride and Prejudice.*

Years of *Dateline* episodes tells me that a man who doesn't use a photo of himself and uses a fake name is going to chop me up into tiny pieces, but as I scan the profile, there's nothing about it that seems desperate to ensnare lonely women or even find 'love.' If this man wanted to deceive me, it seems like he would have used a profile photo of a model or at least used a name that wasn't so clearly fake.

Below his photo is what the website calls the user's *Letter of Promise.*

I receive great fulfillment from being a protecting mentor while also receiving the lust of a lover. I seek the one who has found herself ready for love and discipline. You should know, if we reach a certain level of intimacy, I spank. I hope I have eliminated most of you from my profile now, I loathe wasting time.

I cover my mouth to stop myself from laughing. At least he's straight-forward and has a sense of humor.

My hand hovers over my laptop's touch pad. I should definitely skip over this guy. I should find another decent guy like that pediatrician and just settle down. I've already had a lifetime of reckless behavior, determined to feel adrenaline pump through me. I can settle now. I should definitely settle.

Discipline.

I squirm in my chair. In college, when I was still

getting high, I hooked up with this guy who used to grip onto my hair whenever we hooked up. He never lasted long, but there was always something sharper than adrenaline that charged through me every time I felt that sting of pain. I liked it a lot more than I cared to admit.

I can just meet this guy in a public place. I'd like to think I'm a good judge of character. He won't know where I live. He won't be able to kidnap me and I won't become a topic of *Dateline* a year from now. There, I've justified it in my mind now.

I click on the tiny envelope next to his name and the nervousness that flares in my stomach is exhilarating. A screen pops up with the words *Your Letter of Love* written above a blank box.

I type into the box: *I am naturally submissive. I like the idea of putting myself in the hands of another whom I trust. I'm not saying that would happen right away, but could with the right man. I'm willing to meet.*

I click send, then quickly minimize the screen. He's probably a creep. I'll wake up tomorrow with 200 dick pics and have to shut down my account.

I run my fingers through my hair, tugging on the strands before I let my hand fall. Still…this is what I might need to get over Finn Garrett and get Erin off my back at the same time.

I reread his description. I imagine his hands on my ass, the cold breeze of air after he lifts his hand away, the sharp rise of heat as his hand comes down and my flesh ripples under his palm. The sting. The flicker of embarrassment, the feeling of being so completely under someone's control that I don't have to worry about anything except the physicality of it all, and trusting someone so fully that I wouldn't even tense up before the strike.

But when I imagine the man pulling me toward him for a kiss, all I see is Finn Garrett's face.

Chapter 5
FITZWILLIAM DARCY

I'm dying of thirst.

My lips are dry, my throat is parched, and my tongue feels like a piece of numb bark in my mouth.

I'm in Torv Global headquarters, behind a line of six people waiting to drink from the water cooler. When I finally reach the cooler, the plastic water jug is empty. Not a single droplet of water will come out. I'm ready to break down crying, wasting the precious water left in my body when Finn Garrett walks up to the water cooler and holds my cup under the spigot. I watch as water pours in. He takes a sip from it, then offers it to me. I reach out for it, only to discover I have no fingers.

It's not a weird or grotesque thing—it's nearly cartoonish—as I realize my fingers have popped off and fallen between the two of us.

Finn doesn't seem repulsed or even concerned. He steps over the fingers and holds the cup to my lips. The water tastes like it came from a water spring untouched by human or animal. It's as perfect as Finn's hand on my back, sliding down to my ass.

I wake up slowly. I'm not disappointed—at least, not too disappointed. I knew the dream was too good to be true. It was so simple, yet everything about it seemed perfect.

And now I'm actually thirsty.

I slide my legs off the bed. I turn my clock so I can see it. It's nearly 3 a.m. Everything feels more tender this early in the morning—maybe it's the quiet and maybe it's just because I'm alone.

I trudge my way to the kitchen and fill a glass until the water sloshes over the edge. I drink from it until it's empty. After I put the glass in the sink, I shuffle back to my bed trying to remember the last time I had my ass grabbed but I give up when it becomes too long ago to be anything but depressing.

As I'm nearly in bed, I notice the green light of my laptop's charger is glowing. I forgot to unplug it, which means I didn't turn it off.

I tap on the touch pad and the screen lights up the entire room. As I'm about to shut it down, the laptop dings and I see a new email notification. I click on it.

You have a new message on Letters of Love

There's no way that guy answered already. But maybe…

I sit down. I click on the message. It's from Fitzwilliam Darcy.

Friday 7 at the Italian place on 5th avenue. I look forward to meeting you.

When I slip back into bed, I think about water. I think about thirst and the way the rest of nature bends to the will of a river. I think about pressure and wetness.

Regardless, I sleep like a baby.

*****

"The ad company pitched three ideas to us—"

"The lab has created three unique flavors for the sports drinks—"

"—For one, we'd be mocking the other energy drinks, with an actor pretending to be super caffeinated—"

"—There's this flavor that's a mix between berry and lemon. Most of the taste testers said it was the worst one. We could drop the lemon flavor but all the other companies have a berry flavor—"

"—but as soon as the cameras turn off, he has to take off this abdominal binder and his teeth are rotting out—"

My typed up notes are a mess. Marilyn is the project manager for the new Torv Vitality energy drinks advertisements and Jackson is in charge of *Torv Global's* newest venture, sports drinks. I was completely unprepared to start taking notes, but Jackson caught Finn in the elevator and Marilyn caught him right after he stepped out of the elevator and they both seem incapable of shutting up or even noticing that the other one is talking. My fingers keep pressing the wrong letters on the company's tablet, so a quarter of the words on my notes have a red squiggle under them.

Thank God it's Friday.

Finn steps up behind me, perusing my notes. He doesn't say anything about them, but raises his hand to Marilyn and Jackson. They both stop talking. He is *truly* a miracle worker.

"Marilyn," he says. "We're not going to go with that ad. Going straight at the energy drink industry will put a target on our backs before we're even off the ground. Tell me about the other proposals."

"They thought we could hire this new singer that's coming up—"

"No."

"Uh, okay. The last proposal was that we go for a more sentimental approach. We start with this classic image of a young father during the Great Depression era. He makes a pot of coffee while talking to his kid. Next, we show the kid as grown up, drinking coffee and talking to his kid. We keep going like that until we reach the present. The father makes a cup of coffee, but as he's about to talk to his teenage son, he sees that his teen son is drinking *Torv Vitality*. The son offers his father one and they drink it together."

Finn nods. "That's not bad. Tell them we want something like that and to give us three new proposals by Tuesday."

He turns to Jackson. "If the taste testers didn't like it, we're not putting it on the shelves. It was a free drink. If they weren't ecstatic about it, that means it's not good. Tell our chemists that there will be a $5,000 bonus for whichever one of them comes up with the best flavor by the end of next week."

"Yes sir. Thank you, Mr. Garrett." Jackson nods before scurrying out the door. Finn turns to me. I feel ridiculously aware of his body—the heat coming off it, the slight inclination of his body toward me, the way his pants slightly tent up between his legs. Since I became disillusioned with my fantasies about Finn, I've tried to focus on the work and picturing him like he's the same as any other boss I've had. Unfortunately, it's hard to draw a comparison between my first boss—a balding 65-year-old with a bulging gut and a wandering eye—to the man beside me, who has a much more alluring bulge.

"What's next on the schedule?" he asks.

I pull up his schedule on the tablet. There are so many meetings scheduled, I'd feel bad for him if I didn't know he has enough money that he could buy a state.

"You have another ten minutes before a car will be here to take you to that new Thai food place down the street, where you'll be having lunch with that journalist, Mark Trada from the *Survival of the Fastest* magazine. They used to be a magazine that just focused on running, but they've expanded in the last year and—"

"—And they wrote an article about me a few months ago that accused me of using patriotism to sell products," he finishes. His hand brushes my shoulder—trying to remove some lint or something equally embarrassing, I'm sure. "Good. You should get lunch now."

"Are you going to set the record straight to Mr. Trada?" I ask, taking off my glasses and setting them down on my desk.

"I'll tell him to put a hundred American flags on my article and belt out the anthem for him." He runs his hand through his dirty blonde hair, making it stand up in various directions and making me think of how he wakes up in the morning. "But, in all honesty, no, I won't say anything. If he believes something like that when there's no evidence of it, there's no amount of evidence that will change his mind. It's not my problem."

"Then why set up a meeting with him?"

"We sell our products in the magazine he sells and he asked Mr. Torv. Mr. Torv is the one who asked me to do the interview, so I am. There's no point in being angry about it. Anger is only useful when it pushes you forward, not when it drags you to the past."

He takes the tablet out of my hands and lays it on the desk. With him so close to me, it takes all of my self-control to not reach up, touch his cheek, his arm, his chest. Any part of him, honestly. "It's been a long morning. Go to lunch. We've had a busy week. At the very least, you deserve the break we're legally obligated to give you."

"Okay." I grab my bag, fiddling with the strap. "Um, you know you deserve a break too. We could push back the meeting after lunch—"

"I appreciate your concern, but, no, we can't," he says. "I told Ms. Murphy I would look over numbers with her and I'm going to. Don't worry about me. I can handle myself."

"Of course," I reply and then count ten awkward seconds as I wait on the elevator doors to open. "I'll see you soon then."

As I get onto the elevator, my phone starts to vibrate, clacking against something else in my bag. I dig it out. It's Erin.

"Hey," I answer.

"Hey," she echoes. "So...your date is tonight. How're you feeling?"

"Like I haven't had time to think about the date."

"Have you chosen what to wear yet?"

"It's a fancy restaurant. I'm not sure. I was thinking the red dress—"

"That's always a solid choice."

"But it has the plunging neckline."

"That's why it's a good choice."

The elevator doors open and I step out. "Erin, listen, I didn't tell you everything that this guy had on his profile—"

"You actually told me nothing except that he didn't have a photo of himself, he didn't offer his real name on his profile, and you had a date with him tonight."

"Yeah, but…well, it's just that I feel like I need to get this right. I would hope that my clothes wouldn't make him run out of the restaurant screaming, but I still want to look like…Kate."

"Who's Kate?"

"This model that's in love with Finn," I say.

"Ah, your boss again."

I step out of the *Torv Global* building. "Oh come on. I don't talk about him that often."

"Sure," she says. "Whatever helps you sleep extra good at night."

I walk around a puddle in the parking lot. "I was thinking maybe I should just stick with—"

The horn is so loud, my mind jumps to the thought of fog horns and my body freezes. In my periphery, I can see the delivery truck coming as I feel an arm reach around my abdomen, jerking me back so quickly that I stumble against a firm, muscular body. The moment I take a breath—possibly the deepest breath I've ever taken in my life—I inhale Finn's woodsy scent.

This is the moment that I know I'm beyond any form of help. From the way my heart feels, I might as well have been knocked out by the truck.

"Are you okay?" he asks in a slightly raised voice. His hands brush down my hair, cup my face for the shortest second and those blue eyes strip me of any breath, thought, or speech. He takes a step back. "You should be more careful."

There's a playful smile on his face, but his voice is firm—almost commanding. Scratch that, it *is* commanding but it's completely natural without being loud or forced. I'd do anything that voice told me to do.

"Y-your car," I say, my brain fumbling to find something halfway-intelligent to say. "It's not supposed to be here for five more minutes."

"If I'm going to kill a few minutes, I prefer to do it outside," he says. "I spend an inordinate amount of time in offices."

"Of course," I say. "That makes a lot of sense. Thank you! Thank you so much Fi–, Mr. Garrett. I'll see you later. Tomorrow. Yes."

I step straight back into the parking lot without looking. I check both ways while I'm already standing there, then look back at Finn.

He raises an eyebrow at me. I feel heat rise into my cheeks, but I like it. I don't know if it's his protectiveness, the heroics, or the fact that he can send all these emotions crashing through me at once.

"Hello?" I hear Erin's voice through my phone. I put it back up to my ear.

"Sorry," I mutter as I walk the rest of the way to

my car. "I wasn't watching where I was going."

"Are you alright?"

I look over to the west, where Finn has stopped to talk to someone.

"Yeah," I say. "I'm alright."

******

Niccolò's Colosseum is a restaurant that's tucked between a bookstore and a toy store. From the outside, it's only notable for the chipped and cracked brick walls, along with the smell of garlic and tomato sauce drifting into the street. But the moment I step in, I know I'm out of my depth.

The tables are covered with white cloth and the wood chairs have designs carved into the backs. The bar is made of black marble and a copper-colored wood and the stools have brown cushions that appear to be made of leather. There are tiny crystal lights hanging from the ceiling.

"Good evening," a maître d' says, standing behind a rustic podium. "May I ask for the name for your reservation?"

I tug on my red dress, the hem seeming a little short for a place so elegant. "Um, I'm not sure what name it's under..."

To his credit, the maître d' remains impassive, though I wouldn't be surprised at this point if he thought

I was a hooker. It's the only sensible reason I wouldn't know who I was meeting here.

"Can you look under Darcy? Maybe Fitzwilliam?"

If he knows *Pride and Prejudice*, it doesn't show on his face. "We have a reservation for two under Mr. Darcy for 7 o'clock."

"I know I'm a bit early," I say. "But is it possible for you to seat me now?"

"It's not a problem, Miss. Your table is ready."

He indicates for me to follow him and I do. He sets a menu on a booth in the corner of the room. It looks large enough for six people.

"This was a reservation for two, right?" I ask. "I just want to make sure I'm getting the right Darcy table."

"It's the only Darcy table," he says. "Mr. Darcy specified this table."

I nod. "Oh, okay. Thank you."

"Would you like to order your drink now or do you need a few minutes?"

"Could I just get a glass of Pinot Noir?"

"Absolutely. We have an excellent selection. Our wine list is right here."

"Um." I pick up the list. "Can I just get whichever one is cheapest?"

His face remains stoic even as I can feel heat creeping into my cheeks. "Of course. I would be happy to get that for you."

He turns and leaves. I sink into the booth, pulling my bag off my shoulder. The reason I came early is because I didn't want to be the kind of woman that looks lost as she tries to find the man she's supposed to be meeting, but I'm starting to think that it might have been better with Fitzwilliam Darcy here. He would have known what kind of Pinot Noir to order.

I pull a book out of my bag—*Pride and Prejudice.* I figured, at the very least, it could lead into a conversation about why this man chose the name of a literary character from this book, but I also love the romance of it all and I don't think anything could calm my nerves like a book I know better than any other person.

Time becomes insignificant as I read about Darcy proposing to Elizabeth. I barely notice the glass of wine appear. It's such an intense scene that I don't notice anything until there's someone leaning over me and someone's hand on my shoulder.

I look up and drop the book. I attempt to stand up, only to realize the table forces me to remain on my ass.

"Mr. G-Garrett," I say. He removes his hand from my shoulder, raising his eyebrow at me like he had earlier today. "How are you doing?" are the words I force out of my mouth. "Are you meeting someone here?" Another beautifully articulate statement showing him I have a keen grasp on the obvious.

He laughs. "Yes. I am."

"I didn't think you had anything scheduled tonight. You didn't have me schedule anything, did you?"

"No," he says. "I didn't. I'm here for personal reasons."

He keeps looking at me. I run my hands over my hair, making certain there's nothing ensnared in it, and then I run my tongue over my teeth. He picks up my book and thumbs through it.

"I've never read this," he tells me.

"No?" I ask. "It's very good."

"Yes, my mother loved it. They've made a hundred movies based on this book and she owned every single one of them. She loved Mr. Darcy," he says. "That's why I chose to use his name."

Chapter 6
COMPANY HANDBOOK

"What?" I ask, the word echoing in my head.

What?

What?

What?

"Fitzwilliam Darcy," he says, sliding into the booth across from me. "It was my mother's favorite character."

"You're...you're the one I'm meeting tonight."

"Yes." He picks up one of the menus as the maître d' sets a rocks glass down, filled with a rich amber liquor. "Thank you, Mr. Thompkins."

"It's my honor, sir. Would you like to order now or do you need a few minutes?"

"Give us a few minutes please, Mr. Thompkins."

"Absolutely, sir. Take as long as you need."

I stare at the back of the maître d' until he turns around a corner. I switch my gaze to my wine, pulling the glass closer to me. I try to remember what I had messaged to him, but my brain only seems capable of feeling embarrassment now.

"Despite your great shape, I surmise that you're not a salad girl," he says, still looking at the menu. "I'd recommend the Delmonico ribeye."

I slide my hand across the table, grabbing the menu. I open it slowly, holding it up to hide my face.

What?

My heart is beating so hard and I have to remind myself to breathe. Part of it is ecstasy—he *knew* I'd be here; he set up this date knowing I'd be here, and now, *we are both here*. Haven't I dreamt about him fulfilling my thirst? Haven't I dreamt of him leaving his mark on me, so I can finally have some proof that maybe the way I feel toward him is mutual?

Still, nobody at *Torv Global* would be okay with this. And what if things end badly? It's completely within Finn's power to blackball me from every decent job in New York City. My life has been full of bad decisions and I can sense myself hurtling toward one right now.

"I've heard their fish is good too, but I'm not a fan of fish other than sushi, so I couldn't tell you my personal feelings on it." He sets the menu down. "If you have questions, you should ask them now."

"Why?" I finally blurt. "You could have just asked me out. You could have used your real name on your profile. Hell, if you used your actual photo, you'd get a million messages."

"And if I used my name, I'd get even more than

that," he says. "I've had that profile for a few months now. I don't show my face or use my real name because then I'd have a million gold diggers begging me to talk to them. My interests are a bit more exclusive than that."

"Your interests?" I ask, raising my glass to take a sip and then barely saving myself from strangling as I can barely feel the difference between swallowing and inhaling at the moment.

He glances up at me. "Yes. That's why you replied to my profile, isn't it? Because the way you said that you liked putting yourself in other hands was enough to pique my interest."

I nearly spit out my wine. "Are you really going to bring that up here?"

"I can't exactly bring it up at work. I also brought up the food and you didn't seem interested, so we might as well skip the small talk."

"It's against company policy," I say, though I'm not entirely certain this is true. The company handbook was nearly a hundred pages long.

He leans back. The way he moves makes me think of a lion, muscle and control enshrined in one body.

"I'm aware it's against company policy," he says. "And if that's your choice with how to go forward with this, then I have no problem respecting that. But I know that the way you want to be treated and the way I want to treat you isn't easy to find. And maybe we aren't compatible in that way, but I have no desire to continue looking for something that I've already found. Do you?"

A waiter approaches the table. While the maître d' looked old enough to be my grandfather, the waiter looks young enough to be someone's kid brother.

"Good evening. My name is James and I'll be your server tonight. Are you ready to order?" he asks. Finn keeps his eyes on me. I nod once.

"I'll get the Delmonico ribeye. Medium," I say.

"I'll get the porterhouse, medium-rare," Finn says. We hand the waiter our menus, he thanks us, and leaves. Finn sits up straighter. "Good choice of steak."

"You recommended it," I say. "And I like having a man in control of a situation."

He smiles. "Good. I enjoy being with a woman who trusts me enough to give up control."

"So, how are we going to do this?" I ask.

"Discreetly," he says. "The only reason I was willing to come here is because I tip everyone enough at this place that they don't feel the need to gossip and everyone else here doesn't come to check out other people's tables."

"It's a very nice restaurant. But I still don't get why you didn't tell me that you were meeting me. We spent all day together."

"Maybe I wanted to catch you off balance. I find you irresistible when you're blushing," he says. As if on cue, I feel my cheeks burn. He smiles again, taking a swig of his drink but keeping his eyes on me. "So, we will act professionally at work—or at least in front of other people. We'll avoid being in any public place outside of work. I have your number, so when I need you, you'll come…to me. Like you already do."

"Yep," I manage to say and then start to correct myself to say *yes sir,* but don't get the chance.

"I do need to know some things first."

"Okay."

"Are you actually experienced in being submissive?"

"Do you mean have I been submissive in other relationships?" I ask. "Um, not…like what we're talking about."

"Then how do you know it's what you want?"

"Because it's what I…think about when I'm fantasizing."

He nods. "Okay. What about a safe word? Do you have one in mind?"

"What about Delmonico?"

"You want a four syllable word for your safe word?"

"Right. That was stupid. Sorry." I bite my lip. "What do you think? What would be a good safe word?"

"*Apple* is a classic," he says. "But *stop* is also another classic."

"Apple is good."

I take a sip of my wine. My mother used to tell me that I had no sense of self-preservation—as a child I'd run into the street without looking and talk to strangers without a care in the world. I'm older now, a little more wary of strangers—I'm even wary of some people I've known for most of my life—but this feels less like danger and more like returning home. What I learned as a child is that it was okay to toe the line of danger, but only when there was someone trusted nearby. Inexplicably, maddeningly, and wholeheartedly, I trust Finn.

******

Marge shuffles toward me, holding the tablet in her tiny hands.

"So, while you type, you want to have a code. You don't need to type out whole sentences or anything like that. If that young man...the one with the pale skin...if he is telling you about the decrease in demand for dumbbells, you just write 'd' for down and 'bell' for dumbbells. You should know what you're talking about later to tell Mr. Garrett and if he wants it emailed to him, you can just type it out."

I help Marge onto her stool. Someone in Torv Global didn't think I was doing the best job as an assistant and brought Marge in to train me. It's a bit humiliating, but it's made worse by the fact that Finn seems to be outright avoiding me now.

"Now, you mentioned sometimes hitting the

wrong keys when you're trying to type quickly," Marge continues. I see Finn enter the room. I keep him in my periphery but pretend to be focusing on the tablet in Marge's hands. "You're just going to have to keep practicing. Practice, practice, practice. It's not just for little league teams."

Finn is walking straight toward us now.

"Thank you, Marge," I say. "You've been very helpful."

"Marge, Sarah," Finn says. We both look up at him. "I'm going to that lunch meeting I have with Daniel Wright and Emily Chance."

"I was just about to remind you, Mr. Garrett," Marge says, turning the tablet screen to show a pop-up that says *lunch meeting 11:45.*

"You're the best, Marge," he says, giving her shoulder a small squeeze as he passes by. As he walks away, I watch. I see him pull his phone out of his pocket—his thumb moving so quickly across the screen, he could only be texting someone. When I look back at Marge, her lips are slightly pursed together and I can practically feel the weight of her gaze. My phone vibrates on my desk. We both look down at it and I thank God that it's face down.

"I was just thinking about his meetings after lunch," I explain. "I'm just running through it in my mind."

"It's none of my business," she says, her voice a

lot curter than it had been a minute ago. I step closer to the desk, hiding my phone behind my body before I grab it.

"I'm just going to…run to the ladies room," I say. She doesn't respond, looking back down at the tablet. I hurry down the hall and into the bathroom. I go to the last stall and lock it behind me. My nerves are all over the place, my heart beating so fast that I feel like I could faint. I shouldn't be this nervous over a text, but I know it's him. I know what it could mean.

The phone number is unknown. I slide to the right on the notification and the text flashes onto my screen.

This is Finn. I'd like to see you Friday at 7. I will pick you up at your place. What is your address?

It feels like there's a butterfly in my chest and a butterfly between my legs. It feels like I'm a sixteen-year-old girl again, aware of the hype around sex without ever having been touched before.

I send him a text with my address. No assent, no question about what we're doing, no pleasantries. He has me wrapped around his finger and I like it.

Chapter 7
NEW RULES

I check the mirror again and then pull my hair out of its bun. It tumbles onto my shoulders, still slightly damp from the shower. I had put a subtle amount of make-up on and it takes nearly all my self-restraint to not put on enough make-up to put models to shame.

I run my hands over my black dress—slightly longer than the red one, but strapless and more formfitting. I consider it my lucky dress.

I bought it a couple years ago from a boutique but I've never worn it before. It just seemed too beautiful to risk deterioration from use or staining it with something.

But tonight will be the first night I knowingly go on a date with Finn and I want to look flawless.

I don't look flawless. I look like myself in a nice dress.

My doorbell rings. I run my hand through my hair one more time before opening the door.

Finn, of course, *does* look flawless. With his dirty blonde hair and five o'clock shadow, he looks like he should be on a California beach, carrying a surfboard with ease with his muscles on full display.

I'd travel to the West Coast to see that. I'd quit my job, buy a plane ticket, and live under a bridge to see that now.

"Wow," he says. He reaches forward, his fingertips brushing against my hip for the briefest second before they grab onto me, pulling me toward him. When his lips touch mine, I'm overcome by the feeling of my heart—the pounding inside my chest, the whoosh of blood, the heat it gives off from so much activity. Then, his hand moves under the hem of my dress and all I can think about is my skin, the way it feels every little thing and how amazing it is to feel every little thing. He is kissing me. We are kissing! To say it's surreal is an understatement.

And I just want him over me like a blanket, like an ocean tide, like a heavy, heavy secret.

I hear him close the door with a swipe of his hand, but he still has one hand on my waist and his mouth is still on mine.

"Show me your bed," he says, his voice hoarse but as commanding as it is at work. As we cross the threshold to my room, he grabs my hips, pulling me hard against his chest with my ass pressing against his groin, where I can feel the heat and girth of his arousal. He grabs my jaw, turning my head and he kisses me, harder than before.

This is happening! Like make believe turning to life, a picture from a coloring book pushing itself up from the page and into the three dimensional world. Holy shit!

I want to feel his skin on my skin. I want to feel him, his heat, his pleasure, and I want all of that for me too. I just want him to be the one to take it and give it back.

His hands move back under my dress. He pulls it up, stopping as his hands move to my breasts. His thumb brushes against my right nipple. I push my ass against his cock. He takes the cue and unzips the dress in the back. It drops by our feet.

He pushes me forward. I stumble, using my hands to stop myself from face-planting onto my bed. The slight chill of being naked is remedied as Finn steps close to me again, our legs bumping against each other, and I feel his hand on my ass. His hands move over it like he's admiring an artifact.

I'm ready for him to take control, to show me the extent he will go to in order to make me his own, to dominate and punish me while leaving me feeling like a cherished princess exhausted on the floor, but instead of the sharp sting of a slap, I feel his lips brush against the small of my back and hear a small clatter as his pants and belt drop to the floor.

I turn, determined to be as sexy cool as the dozens of models I'm sure he's slept with, but any hope of remaining composed is killed as I see his cock. Through his pants, I thought his cock felt thick, but actually seeing it makes me realize I underestimated by quite a bit. The only reason I'm not squirming away in fear of pain is because I'm so wet at this point, it's nearly embarrassing.

As I feel his cock at my entrance, I spread my legs a little wider.

His fingers brush against my slit as he positions himself. I take a quick breath as he shoves into me.

It's sudden with flickers of pain from his size, but as he thrusts into me, any thought of pain disappears. Its replacement—desperate, desperate need—consumes me instead.

Nothing matters but the two of us.

I buck back against him, meeting his thrusts. He grips onto my hips so hard that if we had been in any other circumstances, I'd feel the faint bruises already. As I move my hand down, to reach toward my clit, he grabs my wrist, pins it down onto the bed.

I could feel everything in my body spiraling toward a precipice. I have never come this fast, even with the help of a vibrator, but I know it's coming. I know I should tell Finn, but my body feels like a single nerve or a million nerves intertwined and all I care about is jumping off the cliff and feeling that relief pour over me.

His thrusts become more insistent. Then, his hand

moves from my wrist to hip. I think about his profile—about spanking and discipline. Just the thought is enough.

Every muscle in my body seems to tense as my pussy throbs, squeezing Finn's cock. As pleasure surges through me, Finn thrusts into me to the hilt and I feel his hot seed fill me in pulses.

Our breathing is jagged, but the rhythm helps my heart slow down. He pulls out of me, helps to pull me farther onto the bed and lies down beside me. He kisses the base of my throat.

Somewhere in my mind, I know we have a reservation, I know we had plans, and I know our future is somewhere between dubious and impossible, but I roll onto my side, getting closer to him. I rest my hand on his chest. I feel his heartbeat and know that in this very moment, he is mine.

*****

I wake to the sound of a beeping cell phone. I open my eyes, though I know it's not mine. I turn to see Finn, his chest rising and falling as he sleeps. He's still wearing his shirt and somehow it's mostly wrinkle-free.

I resist the urge to touch his face. I glance up at my clock. It's only 1:53 a.m. Too late for our reservation and too early for any rational person to be calling.

I crawl to the edge of the bed, leaning over to grab Finn's pants. I find his cell phone in his pocket. By the time I pull it out, the screen is flashing *3 missed messages*. His wallet falls to the ground and as I lift it, it folds open to reveal his driver's license. I see the year he was born and quickly do the math in my head that adds up to him being thirty-six years old.

"There should be at least one message from the restaurant."

I turn to Finn's voice. He's sitting up already, sliding his legs off my bed.

"I shouldn't have slept over," he says, standing up. "I believe that was one of our rules."

"I think we decided on not sleeping over at each other's places," I say. "I'm sorry. I'm sure I was the one who fell asleep first."

He takes his pants from me. As I watch him dress in front of me, I relive our night, savoring the memory of the Holy Grail that is his skin and the idea of touching it over and over again until I know every part of him better than I know my own body.

"I thought we were going to…do what you had talked about on your dating profile," I say.

"I thought you were pretty satisfied with what we did."

I blush. "Of course. I was. More than satisfied. It just seemed like you wanted to do it and I didn't want to be the reason you hesitated. I'm ready."

"I didn't hesitate because of you," he says. "I just thought it was better to make you wait and I didn't want our first experience to start with you unable to sit down. You are still my assistant."

I run my hands over my thighs. "I understand."

But I don't.

He leans toward me as if he's going to kiss me, but he grabs his phone from my hand instead. He touches the screen a few times—finding out whose calls he missed. He looks up at me.

"Don't forget about calling Mr. Carter tomorrow morning. I need him to sign that contract."

"Of course," I say. "I won't forget."

"I'll see you in the office."

"Okay."

As he leaves the room, I'm overcome by the sensation of being in an empty room. There's too much space and not enough heat. I suspect it is simply the feeling of being left alone in the middle of the night.

******

Finn is missing.

Technically, he's not *missing*. Marge told me he went to Toronto in the hopes of making an acquisition of a growing Canadian company, but I can't get ahold of him. I texted on Monday—to ask him what he's going to do about one of the company's investors who was arrested for assault. I texted again later in the day to see if he had missed my message. I texted on Wednesday to tell him there were rumors that the Chief Technology Officer was being poached by one of our competitors. Yesterday, I called him, pretending to have an emergency concerning a sudden rise in the cost of printer ink—nothing. It's like I slept with a very corporeal ghost.

"Sarah," Marge says, shuffling toward me with a basket that seems to be full of chocolate and tiny bottles of alcohol. "Look what Mr. Garrett bought me. Isn't it great? Two things I love!"

"It *is* great," I agree as she sets it on the desk. "Did the courier deliver it? I'm still waiting for a package from the Chief Marketing Officer. Harmon, isn't it?"

"Yes, Mr. Harmon is the CMO," she says. "But, no, Mr. Garrett gave it to me."

I sit up straighter. "Mr. Garrett? He's here?"

"Yes, he's downstairs," she says, her eyes watching my body language a little too carefully. I slump down into the chair again, trying to imagine Finn as my boss instead of someone who makes my blood pump too fast.

"Oh," I say. "I just wanted to know because of the printer ink."

"We ordered more yesterday."

"Yeah, but...clearly we're using more than we used to and maybe we should keep track of it."

I hear the scrape of the elevator doors. I glance up to see Finn—like a blonde James Bond except without the pretentious suit—walking out, toward this room.

I could be angry, I could be happy, I could be a mess. I don't know. I feel them all. He should have answered my texts and my call, but just seeing him makes me feel his hand on my ass, the way his body felt against mine, and the fact that every time I'm around him, I feel renewed. So I'm happy even though it irritates me that I am.

He walks straight up to the desk, tapping two fingers on the edge of it.

"Can you call *The Savor Bowl* and make a reservation for six people for tomorrow at seven?" Finn asks me.

"Sure," I say like an idiot. Marge beams at him like he's her grandson that just single-handedly won the World Series.

"Thank you so much for the basket, Mr. Garrett."

"I know you've been stressed with your husband," he says. She hugs him and he pats her on the back before retreating to his office.

Okay, the angry part of me is starting to beat the other emotions now that he's out of my sight.

I call *The Savor Bowl*. At first, they tell me they can't make another reservation for another three months, but I drop Finn Garrett's name and suddenly they absolutely have a table for six tomorrow at seven and I should tell him how much they "look forward to seeing him."

Then again, maybe it wasn't Garrett's name that helped me—I absolutely said 'sex' instead of 'six' a couple times and maybe they thought I just needed to get laid. Sure, that's it.

And I do.

Either way, it's definitely Finn's fault.

I stand up as Marge is lining up the tiny bottles of alcohol on the desk. I'm fairly certain that if anyone was so proudly displaying alcohol in this office, they'd be fired, but the two employees I overheard at her retirement party were right—Finn and Marge seem to have a mother-son kind of relationship and she's given a significant amount of leeway.

I knock on his door.

"Come in."

I open the door, careful to close it after I step in. I march up to his desk as he pulls his laptop out of his computer bag.

I take a deep breath. "Okay, I know when we talked about our arrangement, we agreed that there would be no strings attached. But I was texting and calling you about work. You didn't even tell me that you were leaving the country. I had to learn from Marge. I'm your assistant and if you can't handle treating me like one, I don't think our arrangement is going to work."

I'm proud of myself at first for saying this bold

thing, but then I replay it in my head, watching myself from somewhere above as a third person and I want to apologize and say something like, "Please punish me for my attitude," followed by bending over. But he'd think I was crazy then, wouldn't he? My brain behaves like two debating children, with one sneering to say "Nu uh" and the other responds with a hard-to-argue-with, "Uh huh."

He opens his desk drawer, as though my words didn't affect him in any way what-the-fuck-so-ever, setting his laptop inside of it.

"I understand your complaint. I'll take it into consideration. But I knew Marge would tell you where I was. It was inefficient to tell you both and you knew what you needed to do while I was gone. Marge kept you busy, didn't she? She said that she had been helping you memorize all of the *Torv Global* employees."

I flush. Everything he said makes sense. I look like a psychotic stalker now. Cue the feelings of neediness. "I see. You're right. Um, I made the reservation. Do you need me to call anyone else?"

"No, Jared, Lindsay, Aaron, and Carrie already confirmed," he says.

"That's only four people. Including you, that's five people. You said the reservation was for six people."

"Yes," he says. "I did. I figured you could come along. Lindsay is part of our PR team, Jared is her husband, and Aaron is the CEO of *UnderTone*. Carrie is his girlfriend. I trust them both, but we can say you're just there as my assistant and it's some kind of reward for good work."

"I don't think anyone else takes their assistant out for dinner."

"They also don't buy their former assistant hotel-size bottles of vodka, but it wouldn't be a reward if you expected it."

"The *Savor Bowl* does have that amazing shrimp scampi."

"And chocolate crepes." He moves around the desk, his blue eyes brighter than anything in this room. For a moment, I think he's about to embrace or kiss me, but he leans against the front of his desk, our bodies barely an inch apart. "Maybe we can do something together after the dinner."

"If you're paying, I plan to eat as much as possible, so I'm not sure how flexible I'll be after that." I instantly regret saying that because I don't want to at all appear that I'm saying his idea was anything but exactly what I want, need, and would crawl over glass to have.

"There's always takeout boxes," he says. "And crepes aren't that filling."

He adjusts his watch on his wrist. It seems like a rite of passage for rich men—owning expensive watches when their cellphones can tell them the time. He looks down at it.

"I have a meeting with the VP in fifteen minutes. We'll talk tomorrow. I'll pick you up."

"You don't think that will look suspicious?" Surely I get credit for showing my dedication to being cautious and discrete.

"Maybe," he says. "But it would look equally bad if I drove to the restaurant while my assistant had to take a taxi. I'm not worried about it. I am the boss after all."

"Right. Of course."

He walks me to the door and I leave his office. I sit down at the desk. Marge is putting all of the tiny bottles of alcohol back in the basket.

"What were you two talking about?" she asks.

I want to respond to her with a harshly toned, "What business is it of yours?" but that's not really me anyway and I remember that since Finn cares about her that I should be extra careful to be respectful. So I smile and say, "I was just asking him about his trip."

She raises her eyebrow, clearly not buying it, but she doesn't say anything. It was foolish for me to step into his office while only intending to talk about our arrangement. I'll have to be more careful.

But, in all honesty, careful is the last thing I want to be.

******

The Savor Bowl is the top floor of *Eternity* hotel

and, somehow, they've made it so the restaurant ceiling and the west wall is made of glass. The New York City skyscrapers look like they are speckled with tiny stars, but I know they're just office lights with some poor employee working well into the night.

The inside of the restaurant seems to be designed to look like the cityscape. The walls are a dark blue, but the tables are covered with white cloth and there are white plush chairs. Everything is absolutely perfect except that Finn and I are the first ones to arrive.

"It's only a couple minutes to seven," I say after the host leaves us. Finn pulls out my chair. I sit down and he pushes me back in with the ease of someone who has done it a thousand times. He sits down beside me.

He looks good in a black tailored suit—expensive-looking, but subtle. As he takes a sip from the glass of water in front of him, I notice the gold cufflinks and gold watch on his wrist. The inner machinery can be seen through the face, reminding me of how everything had to work perfectly for Cinderella to know it was midnight and rush home before the prince realized she wasn't who he thought she was.

"Are you sure they confirmed they'd be here?" I ask.

"They'll be here. They know I'll pay, so they'll be here," he says. "Lindsay will likely arrive on time. Aaron will arrive a few minutes late."

"Because he's always running late?"

"Because he thinks it's an alpha move to have everybody waiting on him."

The host returns with a bottle of wine. "Our best cabernet sauvignon, sir."

"Thank you."

The host pours the wine into our glasses.

"I hope you enjoy it, Mr. Garrett."

"Thank you, I'm sure I will."

The host smiles and leaves. I watch him go.

"I was a waitress for a while," I say. "You'd be amazed at how many people are jerks."

"I work with people who are used to getting everything they want. I'm well aware of how many people are jerks."

The thought occurs to me that Finn is also someone who gets everything he wants, but I've never seen him be a jerk to anyone. He leans back in his chair. I think he looks especially good tonight. I'm not sure what it is—the blue tie that's a slightly duller version of his eyes, the way his dirty blonde hair sweeps across his forehead, the faint presence of his facial hair that accentuates his jawline. I still haven't figured out his age but he could be a young looking thirty-five who could pass for mid-twenties if he wasn't so sophisticated.

"You're staring."

"No, I wasn't," I say, flushing. I concentrate on the fabric of my black dress. I thought it might remind Finn of the night we had together, but he hasn't said anything about it. As I'm looking away from him, I see the most beautiful woman striding toward us—blonde, hourglass shape, and a face that somehow reminds me of both Madonna, as in Mother Mary, and Madonna, as in the singer.

She stops next to Finn's chair. They give each other a quick hug and for the first time, I notice a man behind her. He's a few inches shorter than she—which isn't saying much since she seems to be 70% legs—but he's relatively good looking.

"Lindsay, Jared, this is my new assistant, Sarah," Finn says, his fingertips brushing against my arm as he introduces me.

"It's a pleasure to meet you," Lindsay says, shaking my hand. "I'm Lindsay. This is my husband, Jared."

"It's a pleasure to meet you both."

Lindsay turns back to Finn. "I hope nothing bad happened to Marge."

"Her husband has cancer. She's officially retired, but she's still training Sarah. The board thought it was best and you know how those hospital bills can pile up."

"And we both know Marge wouldn't take a handout," Lindsay says. She sits down across from Finn. "Is Aaron hoping to make a grand entrance again?"

"Possibly. He hasn't texted me about any car trouble or anything."

"It's not like he'd actually drive here himself. He

does love sitting in the backseat. Like a child."

The host returns. I watch Lindsay and Jared order their drinks, keeping Finn in my periphery. I expect him to ogle at least a little bit—Lindsay's cleavage is even a bit intriguing to me—but he seems mostly interested in looking at the cityscape.

"So, Lindsay," I say after the host walks away. "You must have dealt with the PR for that investor who was arrested for assault, right?"

"Yes," Lindsay says. "Mr. Stein has been problematic for a while. The man just can't handle his sh—"

"Everybody!" a man in a slightly wrinkled white button up shirt swaggers up to the table. There's a young, short black-haired woman following close behind him. The man pulls the woman out in front of him like a ventriloquist preparing its dummy. "This is Ashley."

"I thought you were bringing Carrie," Lindsay says.

"Carrie," the man—Aaron, I assume—pauses, pressing his fingers to his lips. He raises his finger again like he's lecturing. "Carrie was just an easy lay. Ashley sees that and raises it by also being a real woman."

"You're as charming as usual," Lindsay says. "Sit down, Aaron."

They begin to argue. I look over at Finn. He doesn't even seem to notice that anything is happening.

He drinks his wine, still focusing on the skyscrapers outside as though he occupies this peaceful realm in his mind that he can retreat to at any time in spite of what's taking place around him. Nearly a minute passes by before he turns to the two of them.

"Aaron, you should sit down. The host is waiting to give you and Ashley a drink."

Aaron hesitates but sits down beside me while Ashley sits across from him. This is the most recent demonstration of Finn's remarkable ability to speak softly but to be obeyed by anyone within the sound of his voice as though it were simply how nature intended.

"What do you do, Ashley?" Finn asks.

"Um, I'm an actress," she says. "Or aspiring actress I guess."

Lindsay snorts. "Oh, just like Carrie. That is quite the coincidence. Finn, how many actresses have you dated?"

"I don't date," Finn says, picking up a menu. Aaron turns to me.

"Who are you?" he asks. "You look like you could be an actress. Like a girl-next-door type."

"I'm not," I say. "I'm Mr. Garrett's assistant."

"But you were an actress before that?" he asks. "You know, my company, *UnderTone,* we pride ourselves in making women's undergarments that make them feel like goddesses. You could try on some of our prototypes."

"I'm very happy with the undergarments I already have," I say. I feel Finn's hand brush against me. For a second, I think he just bumped into me, but then I feel his fingertips caressing the skin under the elastic of my underwear. When I turn toward him, his hands are back on the table.

The host returns and looks around at our glasses.

"Sir, miss. May I get either of you something to drink?" he asks Aaron and Ashley.

Aaron glances at the host. "Rum and coke."

"Just water, thanks," Ashley says.

"It's my pleasure," the host says, inclining his head slightly before walking away. Aaron sneers.

"Can you imagine being that old and still having to kiss ass?" he says to nobody in particular. "I bet he'd strip for us for a twenty."

"Oh, Aaron, I didn't know you were into that kind of thing," Lindsay sneers.

"I could show you a thing or two about stripping—"

"Hey now—" Jared stands up.

"Sit down, short stack," Aaron snaps. "You couldn't take me if your life depended on it."

"Aaron," Finn cuts in. "Show your girlfriend a little decency and calm down. Nobody is going to be fighting at this table tonight."

Again Aaron responds to Finn as though insubordination was a concept outside of the laws of the universe. As though Finn was, deep down, in charge.

After Aaron and Ashley get their drinks, I turn back toward Finn.

I whisper, "Why did you invite Aaron and Lindsay together if they hate each other?"

"I wouldn't have invited Aaron if I had known Carrie wasn't coming," he says, glancing over at Ashley. She seems to be trying to ignore her date by perusing the menu.

"I propose a toast," Aaron says, raising his glass. "To being the best in our fields. Or, in Finn's case, the second best."

Finn smiles playfully. "The sales tell a different story." He raises his glass. "But I'll toast to good fortune."

We clink our glasses as a waitress approaches with two baskets filled with steaming hot bread. She sets one basket between Finn and I and the other between Aaron and Ashley.

"Hello, my name is Erica. I'll be your server tonight," she says. She's beautiful with thick brown hair that's pulled back into a French braid. "Can I start you off with an appetizer?"

Finn's hand is on my knee. It's incredibly distracting but wonderful at the same time.

"Ashley, you're new to the group," Finn says. "Do you want to choose one of the appetizers for the night?"

"Um, bruschetta is always good."

"What about you, Sarah?"

"Oh, I don't need to choose anything," I say. "I'm happy with whatever anyone else gets."

"You like spicy food, don't you?" he asks. I rest my hand on top of his. He remembered that I ordered the pasta with arrabbiata sauce on our first date. I guess, technically, our only date. He looks up at the waitress, not batting an eye at her beauty. "We'll get some of the spicy meatballs."

"I'll be happy to get that for you, sir."

The waitress gives us all a smile before retreating back toward the kitchen.

"That was some world class ass," Aaron says, leaning back against the chair. "When I was in Tokyo, those women will just throw themselves at you. And Brazil? My God, you'd think they'd never seen a man before. My cock felt like it was going to fall off by the end of the trip. But American-made ass is always fun. You guys know me—always supporting my country."

"You have to travel to those other countries because you have dozens of factories in them," Finn says.

Aaron waves his hand, dismissing the claim. "That's just strategic management. Americans give me money and I give them cheap bras."

Finn's hand moves up to my thigh, nudging the hem of my dress up. As the conversation descends into organic growth, ROIs, and content marketing, I'm thankful that the tablecloths are so long. The top part of me only shows me leaning slightly toward Finn while the bottom half of me is heating up like I haven't had sex in years.

When the waitress returns, she sets down the meatballs between Finn and me, the bruschetta between Ashley and Aaron, and six small plates in front of Lindsay.

Aaron's eyes linger on the waitress' chest. "Sweetheart, you seem like a bright young woman. Why didn't you go to college to get a better job?"

"I did. I have a Master of Science in Physics," she says. "May I get you anything else, sir?"

Aaron crosses his arms over his chest. "You could be a bit nicer."

She barely glances at him. "Is everyone ready to order?"

"Yes," Ashley blurts. "Could I get the chicken cobb salad please?"

Everyone else orders their main entree—I order lasagna while Finn orders steak au poivre.

While Aaron begrudgingly gives his order, I take my cell phone out of my purse. I pull up my notes app and type into it.

Aaron doesn't seem as trustworthy as you made him out be.

I show Finn the screen. He smirks at me. He leans close to me but turns his head like he's looking at something behind me.

"I said I trusted him, not that he was trustworthy." He leans away from me again, but the mixture of his woodsy scent and his mouth are close enough to my face that I can fully fall into a fantasy where he takes me on this table full of appetizers right now. A few additional scandalous scenes flash through my mind that involve us doing sexual acts without caring that everyone sees and I feel nervous for a few seconds.

Finn sets a small plate in front of me. I watch as he takes an oversized fork off the plate of meatballs and sets it onto the plate. But I'm not the only one watching.

"So, Sarah, you're Finn's assistant?" Lindsay asks. I snap out of my reverie.

"Uh, yeah. Yes."

"That must be quite the adventure," she says. "He's a hard man to keep track of. Like a stray cat."

Sometimes you just have to give a stray cat milk. I think it, but I let it go. I know I should trust Finn's judgment on her and be respectful, but there's a tinge of jealousy that she's in his life at all. And while I might just be paranoid, she, like Marge, has a look in her eyes that suggests she suspects Finn and me to be more than just boss and assistant.

"I've made it quite difficult for her the last couple weeks," Finn says. "That's part of the reason I brought her here—a bit of a reward."

"You know, Finn, most people are happy just

getting money."

I cut into the meatball. Steam rises out of it. I mix it with the sauce and take a bite. The spices bite into my tongue, but it's better than anything else I can remember having eaten.

When our meals arrive, my lasagna looks like it was cooked in a large casserole dish and the whole thing was slid onto my plate. Everyone else's dishes are just as large in portion.

Everything is going well until Aaron's glass is empty. He starts by twisting around, looking for our waitress. A second later, he raises his glass and begins shaking it, so the ice clatters against the glass. A few seconds pass before our waitress comes running over. Her cheeks are flushed. She tries to take the glass from Aaron, but he keeps a tight grip on it.

"Say please," he says tightly.

"Please."

Finn stands. He crosses over to the other side of the table. He puts his hand on the back of the waitress in the same way that he did with Kate Andrés and leads her away from the table. Aaron glances over at me.

"We're her customers," he says. "If she wanted to be treated more respectfully, she should have gotten a more respectful job."

"You're..." I shake my head. "You could have at least waited a few minutes."

"I don't wait."

Finn returns to the table, sliding his wallet into his back pocket.

"What happened?" I ask but already have an idea since it required his wallet. He shakes his head, sitting back down beside me.

The rest of the dinner is amazing, though slightly tarnished by the fact that Lindsay keeps glancing between Finn and me. Finn, however, either doesn't notice or doesn't care because his hand manages to get dangerously close to my clit and I can only assume he wants me focusing on the activities we could do after this dinner.

When the check comes, Aaron and Jared both make a move to pay it, but Finn picks it up first. I have no idea how much the bill is—I'd assume a lot since the menu didn't have prices—but I do manage to get a glimpse of the tip he leaves.

"What did you tip her?" Aaron asks.

"A couple hundred dollars," Finn says.

"Are you kidding me? She wasn't that good," Aaron says. "I wouldn't leave her anything."

"I know what you would do," Finn says. "She deserves it. She was attentive and friendly."

"She was friendly to you." Aaron's gaze switches over to me. "I can be friendly too if I find someone worth being friendly with."

The waitress comes by and takes the check with Finn's credit card. As we wait for her to return with the check, I keep glancing over at Finn. I thought he would have been angry about Aaron hitting on me, but he seems completely unfazed.

After we leave the restaurant and I'm putting on my seatbelt in the passenger side of his Mercedes, I turn to him.

"Weren't you a little bit mad about Aaron hitting on me?"

"No."

"Why not?"

"I had no reason to be. You're not into him. Would you rather I made a scene and revealed that we were together?"

"Most men would have been jealous."

"Most men are obsessed with their image."

"You wear a watch that could pay my rent for the whole year."

He glances down at it. "That has nothing to do with image. It's important to me."

I cross my arms over my chest. "Please just take me home." I'm being a bitch. No, I'm not. I know what we are and what we are not but do I not matter more to him than that? I've felt jealous of even a couple of men who turn to look at him, let alone all the women, and he has no reaction to someone suggesting sexual things about them and me – in front of him?

"You're being very moody over the fact that I didn't act like a barbarian in the restaurant."

"You're right, I'm sorry. I didn't want you to act like a barbarian. I just thought—"

He kisses me. Not soft and sweet like in fairy tales, but he kisses me hard enough that I can imagine him leaving his mark. I feel his hand on my shoulders, pulling down the straps of my white dress.

He leaves a single kiss on my shoulder before his hands are suddenly off of me and starting up the car.

"What was that about?" I ask. He pulls out of the parking lot. Nearly a minute of silence passes.

"I had a minute in which I lacked control," he says. "I'm used to being in control, having a grasp of everything that's going on around me. Around you…that seems to waver. That's why it's best that we work as separately as possible at the office."

"Why? Because you think you'll lose control and want to fuck me in front of everyone?"

"Maybe."

"Like, maybe over your desk?"

"Perhaps."

I press my hands together between my legs, ignoring the furious flutter there. The only reason I don't jump into his lap now is because if he rejected me, I'm fairly certain I'd die from inadequacy and lust.

The rest of the ride is quiet. I'm not sure what to think. I watch us speed through the city like we're heading to a certain destination, but I'm not sure that we are. I'm not sure that we'll ever be where I want to be.

Chapter 8
FOR WHAT IT'S WORTH

Marge is great at everything on the company tablet except the calendar app. There's a simple system of sending invites to people and as soon as they accept, it shows up on the calendar app, but Marge doesn't trust it, so there's the largest calendar the world has ever seen nailed to the right of our desk. Any kind of meeting that Finn has with higher management is highlighted in a neon yellow color, anything to do with finances is in lime green, and anything else that's important is in red pen.

Anything that's deemed less important has no color coordination whatsoever. Marge just scribbles it in with whatever pen or pencil she has lying around that is not the same color as the ones above it in the hierarchy.

"Marge," I call her over as she nibbles on cheese and crackers. She shuffles over. I feel some guilt over her working while her husband is sick, but Finn had mentioned to me that she needed the income and wouldn't take a handout. Plus, with the innuendos she tells me about her time with her husband, I assume he's relatively stable. "What does this line say here?"

I point to yesterday's date on the calendar. I hadn't noticed it before because the writing was tiny and the red pen covered up some of the pencil scrawl.

Marge trudges right up to the wall, squinting up at the writing. "Hmm."

Not a good sign.

I wasn't around for the second half of the day yesterday because I had to track down a reclusive app developer—the best in the business, who would only speak to people who had been recommended by one of his past clients—so we could convince him to create a new, innovative fitness app with us.

I ended the day feeling tired but accomplished and now I'm beginning to question whether I should have felt any relief at all.

"Hmm," Marge says again. "I assume it was a meeting."

"I assume it was too," I say. "But when you called me yesterday, you just said the meeting with Ms. Lyle went well. You didn't mention a meeting before that."

"I don't recall...maybe the meeting did happen and I just don't remember it."

"Did you tell Mr. Garrett about it?"

"Hmm."

I truly wish she would stop making that noise and I'm beginning to question whether her retirement was fully dependent on her husband's illness.

"I don't think so," she finally says. I rub my temple.

"Okay, we have to figure out who this person is and call them. We'll reschedule it before Mr. Garrett even knows—"

"Before I know what?" a deep voice asks.

I spin around to see that Finn has walked in, his leather briefcase in his hand.

"Um, nothing," I say. "We were just talking about tomorrow's schedule."

"Really?" he asks. "Because I received a call from an FDA buddy of mine. I wanted to talk to him about some FDA regulations but he had waited for me for half an hour at *Quintessence* and I never showed up. Do you know why that could be?"

Marge steps up, opening her mouth as she looks like she's about to turn into a puddle of tears.

"Mr. Garrett—"

"It was me," I cut her off. "I took the call with your friend, but I got distracted and never wrote it down. I'm very sorry. It won't happen again Mr. Garrett."

Finn glances over at me. I can't read his face. His eyes flash an emotion that I can't define.

"Sarah, come to my office."

I run over the conversation in my mind as I follow him into his office. He didn't seem disappointed or angry, but he never does. He could just be exceptionally good at hiding it.

He closes his office door behind us. He indicates for me to go to his desk. He follows me so closely to the desk that I can feel his knee occasionally bump against my leg. As I start to sit down in the chair across from his desk, he stops me. He grabs my arm.

"Stay standing up."

He takes a step to the left, so he's standing right behind me. There's a thrill in my chest as I can feel the heat of his groin against my ass.

He breathes into my ear. "Weren't you talking about me losing control in front of everyone last night?"

"Yes," I squeak. He moves away from me, toward his desk, and his hand smoothly brushes the top of its polished wood. He sits down.

"Come here."

I stagger over toward him, starting to feel the wetness between my legs.

I stand in front of him. Several seconds pass by while he just stares at me. I hear the air move out of his lungs.

Then, like a lion pouncing, he grabs me around the waist, pulling me onto his lap, my stomach rubbing against his thighs. He swipes my skirt up with the back of his hand and then rips my panties as he yanks them down my legs. I don't even have time to understand what's happening when his hand strikes against my bare ass.

It feels like my flesh was marked with a branding

iron from the heat radiating off. By the third time his hand makes contact, my body jiggling from the force, I can feel that thin line between pain and pleasure and all I want to do is grind up against it, but I also want Finn's permission to do that. I want to give him all of my control and know that he can give me what I want better than I ever could. Whether this is punishment or play, it's his call.

I used to feel ashamed of these things, but when there's enough pain and pleasure in my body at the same time, shame can't occupy the same space.

He increases the severity of the spanking and I gasp, but only with air so as not to make too much noise. I don't know how the sound of his smacks isn't heard outside of his door.

When Finn is done, my ass aches and I can hear his slightly labored breath. He spins me around and puts me in his lap, my sore butt pressing against his legs now. He kisses me, softer than he ever has.

"You are too beautiful," he says. When I don't say anything, he kisses me again. I'm cradled in his arms. We stay like that for several minutes before he tells me that he has another meeting to go to and then kisses my forehead.

I get to my feet and stagger away from his desk. After a few steps, Finn walks with me to the door, his hand on my back to help steady me. I leave his office and he closes the door. I hear the door lock.

"What happened?" Marge frets, shifting weight between her feet.

"Nothing."

"He seemed angry."

"No. He wasn't, really."

I push a finger against my skirt to hold my ripped panties in place so that they don't fall down to my ankles. I sit down at the desk. I can almost feel the bruises blooming and spreading on my ass.

As I lean back, I close my eyes. I remember his hand coming down, the breeze of air before the sharp pain, his palm against my butt, the rush of adrenaline through me. Every time I shift my weight, I feel the sting and I think about it. I think about him. I smile.

"So, he really didn't fire you? You know, I owe you, Sarah. I know that I'm technically already done at this company, but I do need the money and I'd hate to disappoint Mr. Garrett."

"You don't owe me anything, Marge. It was my pleasure."

******

Mr. Ricks, the human resources manager, is nicknamed *The Mammoth*. Polite people will tell you it's because of his impressive mustache, but he is a rather large man.

He adjusts his glasses as he stares at everyone in

the office. Someone—janitorial staff, maybe—had set up folding chairs in the middle of the office and he's giving a presentation using two dolls that resemble voodoo dolls I saw in a documentary a few weeks ago. A video presentation on "sexual harassment in the work place," has just ended and we are all staring at a blue screen.

"So, if a co-worker makes a comment to another co-worker about their, um, body parts, it's sexual harassment," Mr. Ricks continues. "And we should all avoid it. We should all be focused on our work. If you feel any…attraction to one of your co-workers, you should just…deal with it. On your own and in your own homes. Uh…I don't mean that in a sexual way. You all know how it is. Just view your co-workers as co-workers and not as anything else. You might not see something as sexual harassment, but if your co-worker does…well…it could be so just don't do it. Don't even think about it."

Finn isn't attending this seminar. As the CEO, I suppose they think his time is better spent on increasing the profits of the business, but as I cross my legs, causing a shift of weight on my ass, I can feel the faint bruises still on the right side of my ass. It's a good reminder. I've spent nights looking in the mirror, running my hands over my ass, imagining the sharp pain of Finn's quick hand and the heat as my body responds to his power.

"Sarah?"

I snap out of my reverie. Mr. Ricks is staring down at me and the room is full of harsh grating sounds as people slide their chairs across the floor to put them in the closet where they stay.

"Doesn't Mr. Garrett have that meeting with Mr. Kwan this afternoon?" he asks. I glance over at the clock.

"Yes, sorry, Mr. Ricks," I say. "Thanks for the seminar."

"Well, it's not accusing anyone of anything. Especially someone as nice as you," he says, his eyes lingering for a second too long on my chest. "We're just required to have everyone attend."

I can almost hear the rest of the sentence he doesn't say: We are just required to have everyone attend who isn't important to this company.

I return to my desk, setting the pamphlet down that Mr. Ricks had given us and picking up my company tablet. I knock on Finn's door.

"Come in."

I step in, closing the door quietly behind me. When I turn to look at Finn, my heart feels like it collapses into freefall. He glances up at me and I forget to breathe for a few seconds. He is just more than I could ever imagine as a perfect man, but not in the fairytale Prince-Charming way. He's grittier. He's a rose with thorns I like being pricked by.

Beside him is a less attractive man, but still handsome.

"Sarah, this is Mr. Kwan."

"Oh," I say, surprised. I assumed Mr. Kwan would have been older. I hurry over to the two of them and shake Mr. Kwan's hand. "Mr. Kwan, I'm Sarah Moore, Mr. Garrett's assistant. I'll just be taking notes on what is being said today."

"It's a pleasure to meet you," he says. I settle down in the chair near Finn's desk, pulling up the note app as the two begin to speak about a song for the *Torv Vitality* radio ad. They argue about whether or not they should use a popular artist's song or someone lesser known. I can see them both calculating their moves in their mind, trying to get the upper hand in the conversation and it's fascinating to me. Most of the men who pretend to be just as confident and incisive as Finn end up leaving the room, some nearly in tears from frustration or running away with their tails between their legs. But Mr. Kwan is holding up his side of the debate—he's certainly not winning, but he's keeping his cool.

"Sarah, what do you think?"

I glance down at my notes, where I had just been typing what was said but not really paying attention to the meaning of the words. "About whether to use a popular song or an indie song?"

"Yes," Finn says. "When you watch ads, do you

prefer the ones with songs that you already know or a song you haven't heard of, but is still catchy?"

"If the song was catchy, it would have been on pop radio already," Mr. Kwan says.

"I like the indie songs. I'm already sick of the pop songs from hearing them all the time."

Finn raises his arms in triumph while Mr. Kwan shakes his head.

"Come on. She's your assistant. If you said you preferred eating dog food over filet mignon, she'd agree with you." He glances at me. "No offense, Miss Moore."

"None taken, sir." Maybe a little.

"Sarah knows she can tell me her true opinion about anything," he says.

"We both know that you have your beliefs and you hold them close to your heart," Mr. Kwan says. "It's not an insult, Mr. Garrett. It's just the nature of a man who demands the best of those around him and believes he defines what the best is."

"Finn does know what is best," I say and feel a tingle on the back of my neck similar to when I was a little girl and would defend a friend from the mean words of school bullies. "That's why he's so good at his job."

Mr. Kwan glances at me again before standing up.

"It seems that you've made up your mind. My people will send you over a list of potential songs we think would be a good fit. I'll see you later, Mr.

Garrett." He inclines his head toward me. "Miss Moore."

I watch him leave the office. After the door closes behind him, I turn back toward Finn. His hand is following the perfect angles of his jaw.

"You know you shouldn't have called me by my first name to a collaborator like that," he says. There's a flutter in my stomach from his tone. At first the nervousness makes me want to apologize and promise him that it won't happen again. But as seconds pass by in observation of my speechlessness, it takes self-restraint not to beg him to discipline me. I decide not to hike my skirt or bend over to touch my toes so that my ass is as clear a target for him as possible. I take a breath to calm myself.

"I'm sorry," I say, standing up. "I wasn't thinking. He was just being...I don't know, a bit disrespectful and I felt the need to defend you."

"I don't need to be defended."

I take a step closer to him. "I know, I shouldn't have said anything, but—"

"Call me Mr. Garrett."

"Mr. Garrett," I nearly purr. I am standing in front of him now. I reach for his face, wanting to trace along his jawline like he had been doing, but he grabs my wrist.

"I'm going to have to be certain that you remember next time." He yanks me forward and I sprawl onto his lap. His arm moves around me, pulling me tight against his abs. He lifts my skirt and I hear the tear of my panties before I feel the air against my bare ass. If I wasn't a mixture of insane adrenaline-loving scared and adrenaline-loving aroused, I'd be a little sad because those panties were one of my favorites.

His hand comes down with the speed of a guillotine and the force is enough that it scoots my body forward. It doesn't stop him and his hand becomes my heaven and hell. I'm so helpless and it gets me so turned on that I can only assume it's tapped into some evolutionary craving to be dominated or there's something broken in my head that can only be stitched back together with punishment.

After my ass is a red globe, he stops, with his hand resting on my right cheek. He lightly slides his hand in a circle, tracing my butt. The contrast is dramatic since only seconds ago he was wearing it out. The skin there is tender but partially numb from the spanking, which makes this new sensation unexpectedly incredible. I feel electric prickles between my thighs and my existence begins to hang on his movements, as each time his hand ventures to the bottom of my butt, I hopefully anticipate that he will move his fingers toward my middle to fondle a much more sensitive area than my ass.

He turns me on my side, but I am still on his lap, and he moves his hand up to my hair, brushing his fingers through it.

"Can you keep going?" I ask.

"You want me to keep spanking you?"

"Yes. Please," I say. "I just...I'd like it if you did it until I cried."

His eyes search mine and his mouth is curved in the beginning of a frown. "I don't know if that's the best idea."

"Please. At least this once."

His gaze continues to pierce through me and I can imagine him sifting through my thoughts, deciding if I'm capable of handling what he can give me.

"Remember your safe word," he says just before his hand slams down on my ass again. It's harsher and faster than before, almost as though he's angry at me for asking him to do this. It's a raw experience, riding what is apparently a line between agony and a crude need I have that's being fulfilled. I find myself having nearly an out-of-body experience at times, but the pain always brings me back and I revel in it. I imagine it's difficult for anyone else to understand, but there's a thrill in being on the edge of something. There's an animal instinct in me that must miss the brutality of the wild. Maybe I'm overthinking it.

The top of my ass is beginning to feel almost totally numb, but he must be hitting a bruised area underneath it because I can feel a radiating energy in my chest that instantly reaches to my fingertips and toes before extending to my ears which begin to ring. Then, as though an outside force controls my body, air rushes from my mouth in jagged breaths. An audible whimper escapes from my throat that he probably can't hear over the sounds of my flesh being struck and I feel the warmth of tears well in my eyes. As the moisture pools, a tear slides down my cheek, splatting onto Finn's leg, and he stops.

His arms move around me, gently scooping me up around my rib cage and pulling me close to him. He kisses my cheek where the tear fell. He then takes hold of my chin, turns my head, and kisses the other cheek too. I attempt to control my sobbing by resting my face on his shoulder.

Over the course of three or four minutes, my crying quietens into a soothed but deep breathing. I lift from his shoulder and look into his eyes. I reach up and touch his face, my fingertips following along his jawline like I had wanted to before. As the pain fades, I think about how I want to see this face every day of my life and every night before I go to sleep. I want the world of him because I see a perfect blue creation in his eyes.

He pulls me closer to kiss me, full on my mouth like he wants to seal this moment in time just like I do. He lets me rest in his arms and I feel so incredibly blessed that he'd take the time to be with me like this.

It's the perfect moment: intense desire, intense pain, and intense comfort, all existing between us. We now bask in the calm after our storm.

I wish it could last forever, but I know how these things go and they always, always, always go.

Chapter 9
COMPLETE ACCEPTANCE

I don't hear from Finn for the rest of the week. For the first half, he was gone for meetings or had the day off. For the rest of the week, he was out of town, doing something, but nobody could exactly explain what he was doing. Marge only explained it as a business matter. At this point, Bigfoot would have been easier to find.

I pace around my apartment. I think about going to a bar, finding a man to sleep with, but I know it will feel like a weak imitation of Finn at best. And I'll be thinking of him the whole time anyway. Who am I kidding? I'm committed to Finn whether he's committed to me or not. I don't want anyone else.

I tried masturbation, but my usual tricks of rolling my hips with my fingers against my clit isn't working as well as it used to. Not only is there no satisfaction, utterly failing to reach orgasm only makes me more anxious.

I grab my phone, finding the two text messages we had exchanged. I send a quick text.

I'm home with no plans.

I grab my glasses, sliding them on as I sit with a new book and my cell phone to the right of me. I read half a page and glance over at the phone.

What could be possibly be doing that would take him so long to answer?

The obvious reason would be that he's working, but I'm more suspicious that there could be somebody else in his life. Who needs to leave town that often when there's video conferencing?

I know it's just jealousy making a prison out of my mind, but I still can't stop feeling that fear, pounding in my brain like a headache.

I go back to my book but I barely comprehend what I'm reading. All the words seem to rearrange into part of Finn's name or I imagine him saying or doing the things these characters do – only better. I just wish it could all be simple between us.

I've read twelve pages by the time my phone vibrates. I grab it. It's Finn.

I'm two hours away from you.

I don't think. I text back.

I'll meet you where you are.

Seconds ticked away.

Meet me at Francesco's Furniture parking lot.

I text back.

I'm coming.

It is still about an hour and a half away, but I grab

my purse, shove my phone and book into it, and get my keys. When I get into my car, the doubts start to hit me. Every article I ever read about dating said I shouldn't be jumping to do everything that a man wants me to do, but I need Finn. My body craves his body as if our sex caused an imprint on me and when he's gone, all that's left is this empty space. I'd pity myself, but the thought of seeing Finn again gives me a sense of renewal. It doesn't matter how it looks to other people because this is what I want and I've never been so certain of anything in my life.

When I park in the Francesco's Furniture parking lot, nobody else is there. None of the streetlights, but there are still shadows that move as cars pass by and it gives me the feeling of being in a horror movie.

I grab my book out of my purse. I try to concentrate on reading while ignoring the imagery of being murdered in the middle of a parking lot contrasted with the imagery of what Finn can do to me as soon as he gets here.

After several minutes, I'm immersed in the story. Everything comes down to whether or not Special Agent Rivers is correct in his assumptions about the Dunlop Killer. Special Agent Rivers steps away from the safety behind the garbage truck. As he's about to check the van that has just stopped in front of the house, he realizes that somebody has opened the driver's side door of the garbage truck. The killer has known he was hiding the whole time. The killer knows—

There's a knock on my window. I jolt away from it, only to see a gray button-up shirt that I recognize as Finn's. As I open the car door, he steps aside. I jump out, nearly ready to leap up into his arms and hug him like I'm a child who's seeing her father after a long work trip, but I think better of it.

"Did I scare you?" he asks.

"No," I say. "I was just happy to see you."

He raises his eyebrow and I remember that old joke, *is that a gun in your pocket or are you just happy to see me?* I flush, looking behind him. His car is parked a few spots away from my car. I hadn't even noticed him drive in.

"Why didn't you park over here?" I ask, gesturing to the parking spot he's standing on.

"It's darker over there," he says. "At that angle, the passing cars headlights won't be able to see much."

"Because you want to get robbed?"

He laughs. "No, baby girl, it's for us."

His hand rests on my back, leading me toward his Mercedes-Benz. My legs rush to keep up with his movement. He opens the back passenger door. I crawl on the leather seats toward the other side, not even certain that it's what he wants. He follows me into the car, shutting the door behind him. It's more spacious than I expected.

Before I can turn around to face him, he grabs my

hips, forcing me to stay on my hands on knees on the seats.

"Why would you lie to me?" he asks. I search my brain, trying to think of what he's talking about. I actually don't want to lie to him. Not ever. Besides the fact I feel like he would know by just looking into my eyes, I want to stay exposed to him. I want him to know every part of me, inside and out. I didn't lie to him about anything.

"I didn't."

His hand comes down on my ass so quickly, there's a pinprick of pain accompanied by spreading heat. I let out a small noise like a yelp. It's embarrassing. And intense. This is what I came here for.

"You said I didn't scare you. Did you not trust me enough to tell me the truth?"

His hand moves over my ass where he had slapped it. It moves up to my panties, gripping the elastic at the top. He briefly pulls on it, the elastic cutting into my skin, slightly rubbing against my clit. I wonder if he can smell my wetness. I wonder if he's as aroused as I am.

His hand leaves my panties and comes down on my ass again, harder this time. My whole body jolts.

"I don't ask questions to hear myself speak," he says.

"Um, I'm sorry, sir. I, uh, I…I just didn't want you to think you had scared me."

"You didn't think I could handle the truth."

"No, no—" I squeak as two more blows strike my ass. He's focusing on one side. I can feel the promise of future bruises growing on my skin and all I want is for the other side to be treated just as fiercely.

There's a pause between us. He's waiting for me to explain.

"I'm sorry," I repeat. "I'm so sorry Daddy."

His hand moves back to my panties, gripping onto the part that curves around my hips. I bite my lip. I hope he doesn't stop. Maybe I wasn't supposed to apologize so easily. Maybe I'm supposed to be defiant. But I don't want to be.

I feel the knuckles of both his hands against the small of my back as he grips the panties. They rip easily in his hands, falling underneath me like a white flag of surrender. There's a moment of reprieve. I turn my head to look at him. He's gazing at my ass as if he's appreciating a piece of art. I hope he likes what he sees and the thought that he does gives me a genuine spark of joy. As I turn my head back around, I see his hand come down in my peripheral vision.

The car is filled with the sounds of my squeaks and the sound of flesh hitting flesh. The sounds are almost sex-like except more fierce. More wild.

His hand strikes down on my left ass cheek like he's intent on making both sides the same shade of red. I grip onto the edge of his seats, my mind enveloped in the pain with a lingering hope that he leaves me enough of a mark that I'll have some proof that he and I were the perfect pair in this moment.

When his hand rests on my back, my ass feels like it's squatting on hot rocks and my pussy is pulsing with need. I turn around, eager and happy to see him already unbuttoning his pants. As he pulls his boxer briefs down and his erection is more intimidating than I remember it being before, I find myself climbing down in the floor board between the driver seat and the backseats, positioning my head between his legs.

I don't look up at him, but I feel his hand on my cheek, sliding along the curves of my face. I've handed him all my trust and control and, in return, he has given me the chance to be vulnerable and allowed me to break apart while he takes care of every piece of me. I don't have to worry about being wrong or making a bad choice because he makes all of the decisions. As I turn my gaze upward, I know that despite what he's said and despite my own actions, these intimate moments demonstrate a trust between us that's impossible to compare to anything else.

"Can I?" I ask, leaning between his knees. He nods once. I take him in my mouth. There's a faintly salty taste and the heat of him feels good. I run my tongue over the head, but I'm honestly not sure how to do this the best way. I rarely go down on men and the few times I have, they didn't last very long. I switch to kissing the head of his cock, quick and tentative.

He grips my chin so quickly, I barely have time to understand what's happening, but as I feel the pressure under my chin, I rise up a few inches. The slap strikes me across my face so quickly, I jerk back in surprise. It didn't hurt. It was just new. I smile involuntarily and am surprised at how much I enjoyed it. He knew that I would.

"I deserve a little better than that," he says. "And we both know you can do better."

I move back between his knees. I take him back into my mouth, determined to make him happy. As my tongue moves around the head of his cock, dancing over the slit, his hands move into my hair. I slide my hand under his cock to his balls. With my hand underneath them, I create a wave with my fingers and grip them firmly, but gently. His hands grip my hair and the idea that it's enough to please him sends a thrill through me.

His hand moves toward the back of my head. I try to take more of him in, but his cock is bigger than any other that I've seen and my body is less willing to cooperate than my mind, so I just continue to fondle his balls and move my other hand to the base of his cock. I feel his fingertips against my scalp and a wetness between my legs. Once in a while, he makes a small grunt or moan, but remains amazingly self-controlled.

I need to change that.

I work him deeper into my mouth. I ignore my gag reflex, focusing only on getting him to cum. It's big but as our eyes lock, I know I'm close. I've never failed at anything I was determined to accomplish and I certainly won't be starting by making my boss unhappy.

My saliva is making it easier to move my mouth over him. His hands grip onto my hair so tightly that I can hear the ticking of his watch. I feel like it's egging me on, but my hand caressing his balls is getting tired. I try to move it away, but he grabs my wrist, keeping it there. It's enough to motivate me. As I play with his balls, I can feel that growing tension in him. He's a man on the edge of a precipice and it's my duty and my pleasure to make it happen. I honestly don't know who wants it to happen more. I want it. I want to take all he has and all he can give me.

I can feel his balls tensing. I take more of him into my mouth, forcing my throat to relax against my brain's instincts that I'm chocking. It's to the point that I feel his tip at the back of my throat. It feels like one of my best accomplishments. It's only made better by the soft curses coming out of Finn's mouth, his fingers tightening so hard around my hair that his knuckles must be turning white, and then the spurts of warm cum that takes several swallows to get down.

As he pulls out of my mouth, I lick my lips. Of course he would taste good. It's an odd thing to be relieved about, but it's a dilemma I've spoken with to more than one girlfriend. Finn's is a sweet, clean finish that flashes the thought of "yum," through my mind.

I've submissively swallowed him down my throat and into me which is one of the most erotic experiences I've ever had despite the lack of anything touching my vagina. The act itself is complete acceptance of him and the intimacy of still tasting his orgasm in my mouth is indescribable. This is yet another way that his cum has entered my body.

All I can think of is how much I admire him, how much I loved being on my knees for him, and how I would've gladly worked until I physically gave out if that's what it took. I am so damn turned on that it's difficult to inhale fully as I await his instruction.

After he pulls his boxer briefs back on and zips his pants, he pats on the other seat I had been on before. I get onto the seat.

"Lie down," he says and I feel a fresh escape of wetness between my legs at the sound of his command. I lie down, resting my head on his leg. His fingers smooth out my hair that he had crimped with the pressure of his hands. I find myself falling asleep and when I dream, it's our time together tonight, over and over until I've memorized every part and locked it away so that I'll never forget.

******

Finn is coming over.

I've vacuumed the living room four times. No,

five. I've scrubbed the kitchen clean, using a cotton swab to get every small crack. I've cleaned the bathroom with the same precision, frantically scrubbing the shower, though I'm fairly certain he won't ever be inside it considering this is meant to be our time to bond over our love of *The Office*. He's bringing over the DVD set of the first season. I just have to make my apartment look like something worthy of a king. I enjoy feeling as though I'm serving him in this way.

After I shower, dig through my closet to find something casual enough to sit around in my living room, but also that hopefully looks alluring, and get dressed in jeans and a t-shirt (but with my best, lacy bra, and panties that I don't mind being torn), there's still nearly twenty minutes until Finn is supposed to be here.

I sit at the small desk to the left of my TV, opening up my laptop. Erin had texted me, asking if I could send her the photo of me in the park that she had used as my dating profile because she wanted to use it for a birthday gift for my mother. I had cleaned out my computer about a week ago, accidentally deleting the photo, so the only place it could be is on my dating profile.

I wish I had my reading glasses, which I managed to leave somewhere in my apartment. I'd go looking for them, but after all that cleaning, my legs feel like they could fall off. And thinking about my legs falling off just makes me think of having sex with Finn.

Seventeen minutes until Finn is supposed to be here.

I have to reactivate my account on *Letters of Love* since I closed it down after my first date with Finn. All I have to do is log in and it will make my account active again. I guess, despite all of the website's boasts of helping people find true love, they're not too confident in their users finding true love with their first date.

Maybe Finn and I can be the exception. I don't allow my mind to go too far into the future.

Fifteen minutes until Finn is supposed to be here.

There's a sidebar on my profile that shows my exchanged messages. Finn is shown to be the last person who messaged me since deactivated accounts can't be seen by other users and, therefore, they can't message me. His photo of the Siberian Husky is still shown on his profile, which seems strange because I was pretty certain that when someone deactivated their account, their profile photo was replaced by the *Letters of Love* logo.

Fourteen minutes until Finn is supposed to be here.

I click on Finn's name. His profile is still active. There are still those first words that allured me:

I receive great fulfillment from being a protecting mentor while also receiving the lust of a lover. I seek the one who has found herself ready for love and discipline. You should know, if we reach a certain level of intimacy,

I spank. I hope I have eliminated most of you from my profile now.

What the hell? How many more women had responded to that? Jealousy snakes through me, shaking its rattler so loud that it's all I can hear and feel.

Twelve minutes until Finn is supposed to be here.

Of course, I knew spankings weren't just between Finn and me—he had a past, where he must have perfected his craft. But I hadn't thought about him doing it with other women now. I thought it was just us. I thought we were special. I feel like such a fool.

I lean back into my chair, taking a few deep breaths. I can't freak out. There's no proof he's been with another woman. We haven't even had *the talk* about commitment and I don't expect that we ever will. He's my boss. He has more economical and business power than I ever will and he can have any line of women he wants. We were just having a good time.

Still a little peeved.

Nine minutes until Finn is supposed to be here.

I bet he doesn't even come here on time. He's busy. He's not watching time tick by like a desperate housewife, waiting for the delivery man to stop by because the highlight of her day is seeing a man in brown shorts. He could be spanking another woman right now.

I close my eyes. I count my breaths. I feel each one flow in and out of me as my chest and stomach expand and retract.

There's a knock on the door. My heart echoes the knock, then speeds up like I've had a shot of adrenaline. Suddenly, my legs are very flexible and incredibly eager to move.

When I open the door, I momentarily forget all my concerns and frustration as relief courses through me.

Finn reminds me of the ocean with his bright blue eyes and the sandy, dirty blonde hair. I can almost smell the salty, humid air until he moves past me to come in and I'm hit by his own masculine scent. The only thing that offsets this image in my mind is the DVD set he's carrying

I wonder if we truly only have to watch *The Office*. We could spend an hour or two in my small bed, then rest while watching some TV.

"Your profile," I blurt out. He raises an eyebrow at me as he closes the door behind him.

"My profile?"

"Your *Letters of Love* profile. It's still active."

Keep cool. Play it off. Act like you don't care. That's what a model would do. Unless she loved him as much as I do. Loved? I stare blankly at the wall behind Finn. How did I let that word enter my mind. How stupid can I be? It had to be just a filler word my consciousness inserted to describe whatever it is that he and I have. Has to be.

"Yes," he says. "It is still active because I haven't

signed back into the account since you and I met at *Niccolò's Colosseum.* How did you even know I hadn't deactivated it?"

He smirks and raises an eyebrow.

"I needed the photo from my profile. For my friend, Erin," I say. "But...I'm not mad or anything. I was just surprised. I would have thought you'd be...bothered by all the of emails you get from the website."

"Ah. Well, maybe you got tons of emails because of your photo, but my photo was a dog with a very blunt description of what my favorite extracurriculars are. I get an occasional message, but I don't read them. I don't have the time."

"You read my message."

"Yes. I saw your name. I was interested to see if there was more than one Sarah Moore." He indicates over toward my laptop. "I want to show you something."

I nod. He moves over to my laptop, typing in the *Letters of Love* website. He logs into his account. He clicks on the sidebar that shows the exchanged messages. There are several messages in his inbox— apparently, his idea of *occasional* is different from mine, all of them unanswered except for mine. All of the messages above mine were never even read.

"Oh," I say. He moves to the account page. There are two options at the bottom, *deactivate* or *delete.* He presses *delete*.

A message pops up, asking for confirmation that he wants to delete his profile, reminding him that he will lose all information, messages, and contacts permanently. I put my hand on top of his.

"You don't have to do that," I say. "I wasn't...I was just curious about your profile. You don't need to delete it. I'm sure some of those messages are from some very sexy women."

He hits *OK* on the confirmation screen.

Just like an ocean tide crashing down on me, I feel this overwhelming sense of gratitude that's almost suffocating from its ferocity. It's such a small, stupid thing, but, despite my protests, he must have realized it bothered me and deleted it.

Kindness in my life has always come with a price—there's always been an expectation from it, but there's nothing I could give Finn that he couldn't buy or get by himself.

"Thank you," I say. He stands up. As I reach past him to grab the DVD set he had set on the desk, he leans forward and kisses me. It's another tidal wave pulling me under, stealing my breath, but as he pulls away, all I want to do is drown in these kinds of moments. I don't know how long it will last. A neutral third party might give me a certain, unflattering title as to my role in Finn's life. And it's almost always a temporary role. I want to stretch the seconds we're together for all they're worth. I do so against the ominous understanding that the odds are against us and that one day I will most likely look back on these moments with sorrow knowing that they are gone forever. Yet as much as I hate to admit it, I find myself daring to believe that there's a future between us. That we're something more than a shared kink.

"I noticed there's a decent looking pizza place a few blocks down. We should order now," he says. Turning away from me, he looks over the apartment. I could see it through his eyes: tiny, undecorated, and lacking any of the high-tech features that I'm certain his house has. He glances back at me. "You could live in a safer neighborhood."

"Maybe I like the danger of it."

He frowns, but doesn't say anything more. I wish he would. I wish he'd ask me to live with him, but we chose to have this TV marathon at my apartment because none of my neighbors could give less of a shit about who comes to my apartment. Around his house, there are bored housewives and old ladies who would be thrilled to have gossip material about a young woman staying for hours with Mr. Garrett, likely creating elaborate fantasies in their mind to help them get off at night.

I'm meant to stay a secret, but it's hard to be angry about that anytime I see him and when he does things like delete his dating profile when he could easily give me excuses for why it still exists. It's a bit of a dangerous way to hold a secret—recklessly coveting something more overt.

Chapter 10
THE PAST IS NEVER FAR

Working with Finn reminds me of my dehydration dream. There's always this thirst every time I see him— which isn't even that often. Whenever he passes by me to get to his office, our eyes meet and half my brain becomes dedicated to hoping he'll ask me to see him in his office. I need to feel the sharp sting of his slap and the potency of his kiss. But, most of the time, he's too busy, so I cross my legs, tensing my thighs to cause friction against my clit, which only makes me more aroused. I feel like a nymphomaniac—a drug addict, waiting for my next hit, except the hit is literal.

For the last week, Finn has been in and out of the office. Actually, a lot of people have been in and out of the office. There's been some chaos after Kate Andrés, the model for Torv Vitality energy drink, went on an anti-Semitic rant while being high on cocaine, so Torv Global has been focusing on public relations more than anything right now. We've had at least a dozen people come in just to write up an apology/condemnation letter.

Everything is usually completely under Finn's thumb, but this is a reminder that public opinion can get out of control quickly when social media exists. It's also a reminder to me that if anyone begins to suspect that Finn and I are involved, it could cause an uproar about power dynamics and favoritism. In today's nosy world, it seems if any two people are having sex, someone will try to use it to damage them.

You'd think sex would just be the business of the two people having it, but society has given power to busybodies, gossips, and people who don't approve of the type of sex being had as though their approval were needed before any panties or boxers drop. I often wonder if these types of people just aren't getting enough and are jealous of those of us who seem to not only be getting more, but in unique and adventurous ways that they can't even dream of. I often smirk to myself when thinking of what some of the self-appointed judges of sex might think about what Finn and I do. How he spanks me like a little girl in need of discipline for popping her bubble gum in class. It'd probably drive them crazy. Most of them are probably due a good bare-ass spanking themselves for the crime of being prudes. But until that happens, it's a potential threat that lingers in a fog above me. It makes me a bit queasy and I wish Finn was here right now to calm my nerves.

I watch the comments roll in on the company's

social media accounts. The tide is beginning to turn with people realizing that Kate Andrés had minimal connection to our company and there was no way we could have known she had prejudice or drug issues. All in all, she had seemed like a decent role model.

I exhale. Hopefully, this means that Finn will be back soon and he'll have a lot of energy to expel on me.

"Sarah."

I turn without thinking. In the back of my mind, I know it's not Finn. The voice isn't deep enough. But when I see Steve, my heart nearly stops. He has to be a mirage. He has to be a hallucination caused by staring at the computer screen too long.

He walks up to me. He's short for a man, but still has a few inches on me. Stocky, I suppose it would be called and it looks like he's only gained muscle since I last saw him. His brown hair looks greasy, but it could be that he's back to trying gel. It didn't work for his hair, but I never had the nerve to tell him that.

"How are you?" He towers over me as I sit. I want to stand, to be the proud independent woman all the songs tell me to be, but my legs don't want to work. He stares down at me, waiting for an answer.

"Fine," I manage to get out.

"I can see that you've managed to get a better job." He nods down at the large mahogany desk. "How many guys did you have to screw to get this high up at Torv?"

I feel heat rush up to my face, but I don't want him to see. Even if we're not dating anymore, thank God, I'm certain he'd be massively jealous if he knew I'm sleeping with someone other than him. I stand up, but he doesn't move, so our knees hit against each other. His body is too close to mine. I can't breathe with him so near me.

I sidle away from him, grabbing some papers as an excuse to leave. As I'm fully turned away from him, I feel his hand suddenly on my ass, gripping it tight enough that I can feel the faint bruises that Finn had marked me with. I spin around, swatting his hand away.

"Don't," I snap. "How did you find me? How did you even get in here?"

"I told them I was part of a Jewish coalition," he says. "And you were photographed dining with the CEO here and a bunch of other douchebags. The photo mentioned you were his assistant. Funny that you could never get a job like this when you were with me. You seemed content enough flirting with every patron where you waited tables."

"You need to leave."

"Why? Do you want another anti-Semitic scandal on your hands?"

"You're not Jewish!" I hiss. "Please be gone before I get back or I'm calling security."

As I turn away from him again, I know what's going to happen before it does. Anytime I have ever told

Steve to do anything, he does the exact opposite and then acts like I can't take a joke or that I'm being mean to him. But as I feel Steve's fingers again brush against my ass again, Finn appears in my periphery, grabbing Steve's arm before I can even spin back around.

"May I help you?" Finn asks, his grip on Steve's wrist tight enough that I can see Steve's hand turning white. Steve tries to wiggle his wrist out of Finn's grip, but it doesn't work.

"Sorry," he says. "I saw a piece of string on her pants. I wanted to get it off for her."

Finn releases Steve's wrist. "I don't believe you have a reason to be here, so I suggest you leave the premises."

Steve nods once before scuttling toward the elevator. Finn takes the papers out of my hand, setting them back on the desk.

"Come into my office," he says. I swallow, but I follow him in. This isn't how I wanted to be invited to his office. They say you should be careful what you wish for and I never seem to learn that lesson. He leans against the front of the desk and gestures for me to sit in the chair in front of him. I sit, avoiding his gaze. "Look at me."

I glance up at him before looking away again.

"Sarah."

I peer up at him. This may be the last time I can look at that face without him realizing how easily trouble finds me. This could be the last time he sees me as something to be adored and cherished instead of something that has been rotting away.

"Explain."

I cross my fingers in front of me. I could lie, say that Steve was just some random guy that decided to harass me, but from his behavior, he knows there's more to the story. I can't lie to him anyway. He deserves to know the truth.

"His name is Steve Phillips. He's my ex," I say.

"He seems like an asshole."

"He is," I agree. "He's…"

I pause trying to find the right words.

"Did he mistreat you?" Finn asks, the thinnest semblance of anger in his tone.

I press my lips together. There's no way I could say *no* but I didn't want it to sound like I was a victim. "He's a creep. He used to track my phone. He would accuse me of sleeping with any man I had small talk with. He convinced me to cut off all contact with anyone other than him because he said they were trying to drive us apart. When I broke up with him, I…"

I cover my face with my hands. I feel Finn's hand on my shoulder, heavy and warm. I look back up at him, the warm prick of tears threatening to come down. He pulls me toward him, enveloping me in his arms. I press my face against his chest, trying to not cry, but the tears are soaking his shirt anyway. It's so stupid. It was so long ago.

"We'll make sure security has his photo," Finn says. "He won't come back in here. You should give it to your landlord too."

I snort. "My landlord doesn't care."

"I can give him enough reason to care."

There's some comfort in his words, but not in the way he thinks. It's a comfort to know he cares this much—that I'm more than a piece of ass to him. But I know Steve. He's practically a 100-piece puzzle with every piece representing a shitty part of his personality, but the center puzzle piece would be that he's single-minded and obsessive. It's allowed him to be relatively successful as a sales manager, but when his focus was on me, he could have gone through a thousand security measures just to remind me that I was his hostage. I'm certain that his goal coming here was not to harass me but to remind me that he could still devastate my life.

I didn't need the reminder but I'm glad that as my life crumbles apart, Finn can still hold me together.

******

My ass is a bruised apple—in color, shape, and gleam.

Before I had left the office late last night, Finn had asked me to text him to reassure him that I was home safe, but I had forgotten after being paranoid about the feeling of someone following me, so when I got in today, he took me into his office so I'd remember next time.

I stare at my ass in the full-length mirror. I'm not a vain person, but there's something incredibly intimate in the way that my ass has changed to reflect Finn's presence in my life.

My phone vibrates. I check it, feeling that flutter in my chest seeing Finn's name.

Hey, baby girl, meet me at the Pendulum restaurant in The Dusk hotel.

I look back to the mirror. I wish I could arrive late, just to get him to spank me again, but I can't wait to see him.

I peek out the window, the shades hitting the side of my face. That sense of feeling followed—I used to have it all the time, but that was when I was with Steve. Maybe Finn's encounter with him will be enough to keep him away. I choose to live in the moment and hope.

Though, for me to truly believe that conclusion, I'd have to believe that Steve was reasonable and I'm not that optimistic that he had changed so much in the last few years.

I take a photo of my ass and send it to Finn as a reply. He might be my boss and I might be his baby girl—and I enjoy swimming in this sea of lust and submission—but I still hope the image of me can make him squirm a little. I want his attraction toward me to be just as powerful as my attraction to him. When my fingernails scrape down his back, I want to know that I'm taking more of him than just a little bit of skin.

******

The Dusk is a renovated Victorian house with a brick extension that contains the incomparable five-star restaurant. When I walk in, there's the whiff of pine and I'm overcome with the feeling of being in the 1800s. All of the furniture is Victorian and the only thing that stands out is a hostess walking over toward me in black slacks and a white shirt.

"Good evening, ma'am. Are you Miss Moore?"

"I am," I say, though an unsolicited voice in my head allows me to sample the question being asked as, "Are you Mrs. Garrett?" My jaw drops and my vision blurs as I stare at the distant wall. Close to thirty seconds pass until I realize that the server has spoken to me again.

"Ma'am?"

I turn from my trance and make eye contact.

"Please follow me."

When we pass through the ballroom to go into the restaurant, I'm amazed at how shiny the floor remains and how elegant the piano looks. Everything feels so incredibly enchanting—which, I suppose, means it doesn't *truly* feel like the Victorian age or else everyone would have tuberculosis, bad breath, and a corset crushing their rib cages.

The restaurant has dark crimson walls with three large chandeliers hanging from the ceiling. There are only four tables, each are beautifully Victorian— wooden with an ornate base and intricate corners. Each of the chairs are upholstered and the legs seem to be carved to look like claws.

Finn sits at the table farthest away, watching me observe the whole room. Completely ignoring the hostess, I rush over to him. He stands up as I reach him and we embrace.

The hostess steps up to the table as I sit down. "What would you like to drink, ma'am?"

"I'll just get what he's drinking," I say, indicating to Finn's glass.

"Great choice," she says. As she walks away, I keep my focus on Finn, the noise from the other patrons in the restaurant turning into white noise.

"How did you get a reservation here?" I ask. "I heard it's nearly impossible."

"I know the chef. He texted me to tell me there was a cancellation for a table for two and that he was serving his cordon bleu tonight, so I had to come and I had to have you here with me."

He reaches for me, his fingertips sliding down my arm and I feel heat rise from my skin where he had touched. His hand stops at my wrist. His fingers wrap around it, jerking me closer to him. We kiss and I can feel some of his wickedness seep into me. It makes me want to be just as forward as him, shedding off my clothes and creating my half of paradise for us right here on this Victorian table.

The dinner is better than I ever could have imagined. Finn and I both get the chicken cordon bleu. Every bite seemed to melt in my mouth—first, there was the moist chicken, then the salty ham, and the rich taste of some kind of spicy gourmet cheese. I drank wine until my face felt like it was glowing and every few minutes, Finn would touch some part of me like he knew I craved his body. Everything felt endlessly intimate and wide open at the same time.

As our plates are taken away and I'm finishing my glass of wine, Finn stands up and offers me his hand.

"Let's go to the ballroom?"

The slow, sultry music has been seeping into the restaurant, barely heard over everyone's conversations. I would normally avoid anything that required my body to have some level of coordination, but with Finn's hand lingering in front of me, I can't deny him. I take his hand and he leads me to the ballroom.

When we begin to dance, his talent must transfer over to me because my feet only make a few mistakes before we hit a perfect rhythm.

"I didn't know you could dance," I say.

"I've picked up a few things traveling."

What else have you picked up while traveling? The thought ensnares me for the briefest second, but I let it go. This night is too perfect for me to worry about any other woman.

"Well, I enjoy being the beneficiary of your talents."

He smirks but stays silent as we glide across the ballroom floor. Nobody else is dancing, though I can feel some eyes watching us from the restaurant. We exist in our own world right now, where no work regulations or creepy ex-boyfriends exist.

His hand moves down to my waist. "I got your photo."

My brain is fuzzy from the magic of the moment, but my thoughts catch up. "What did you think, sir?"

The last word slips out, a mistake from always referring to him as Mr. Garrett or *sir* during work hours. But he smiles and I know I've done something right.

"I think I've been favoring your right side over your left."

My hand moves to my left ass cheek. I've been shifting my weight every time I sit down, testing the pain from the bruises, and I realize now that he's right. And it's a jolt of pleasure to know he looked that closely at the photo.

His hand moves toward me and as it cups my face, it occurs to me that I'm not afraid of him. Even as his dominance over me is a seed to our pleasure and there are moments of genuine pain, I trust him too much to be afraid of him. Not because he couldn't physically break me in two, but because I trust him. We stop dancing as I gaze up into his eyes.

His thumb moves over my bottom lip. "The colors are compelling. There's mostly blue and red, but the purple creates a real contrast against your skin. It's quite beautiful."

"I agree, sir," I say. "I'm glad we feel the same way about it. It reminds me of aconite."

"The purple, poisonous flower?" He nods. "That makes sense. Beautiful, but dangerous."

"Yes, sir."

He pulls his phone out of his pocket. His finger taps on the screen once and he turns the phone around to show me the photo of my ass that I had sent him. I flush, swatting the phone down.

"Are you trying to embarrass me?" I ask.

"A little. I do like to watch you squirm. And to watch your face turn almost the same shade of red as your freshly-spanked ass." He smirks and slides his phone back into his pocket. "At least it looks like your lesson was learned."

"Yes sir, it was. And I like that whenever I sit down, I feel the sting and am reminded of you. But…" I pause, thinking over everything I want to say. If he decides that I'm too damaged or too much of a freak after I say what I need to say, I don't think I could handle it. I don't think I could find another person as compatible as he is with me. "Never mind. It's nothing."

He rocks back onto his heels. "Tell me."

It's a command, but beneath the curt tone, there's an undercurrent of affection. It's hard to deny him anything.

"It's weird."

"I'm fine with your version of weird."

"Well…" I tuck some strands of hair behind my ear. I wish I could distract him, seduce him into thinking of something other than this conversation, but I know how driven he is. Once he wants something, he's not going to let it go just because it's trying to evade him.

Finn slips his arm around my waist, pulling me tight against his body. He kisses my cheek.

"Just say whatever you need to say," he whispers. "Unless you want me to show these other patrons your photo…"

I know he's joking, but my cheeks still start to burn.

"When we…when you spanked me," I lower my voice and my eyes wander down to his hand that still rests on my waist. "That time I cried."

He nods, his hair rubbing against mine. "Yes, I remember."

"I liked it. I want it to be real sometimes and not just play. And I want to cry in your arms about something minor like that. It seems better than what life can do to me. Does that make sense?"

God, god, god. There it is. It's all on the table. I had plenty of vulnerabilities, but this is one of the biggest ones. If he can't accept this, I may as well resign to a life without anybody. I don't see a future where I could confess this to anybody else if Finn can't even accept it.

I raise my gaze to his face. He's smiling with an empathy I've never seen before and his eyes pierce through me, cutting me down to my core until all that's left of me are the pieces I've never shown anyone else.

He leans forward, kissing me, smearing my lipstick enough that I'm reminded of how he accepts all of my other imperfections.

"Perfectly," he says and I believe him. He raises my arm and twirls me. The room spins and I'm dizzy for a minute. We both laugh and I get as close to him as I can while he holds me in his arms as we continue to dance.

Chapter 11
TO THE GROUND

Finn has been in Italy for nearly a month, trying to woo *Interpretation*, this huge footwear company, into making a new brand of athletic sneakers with *Torv Global*. I'm certain it's great for him—Paris is where models are mass produced—but I'm alone in New York and I just finished an eight-hour shift without him around. I forgot work could be so boring without the anticipation of hearing Finn say my name and not knowing if it was to schedule a meeting or to see my ass ripple under the force of his hand.

I slump down onto my bed the moment I reach my room. Exhaustion has tailed me like a clingy child for the last couple of days. Maybe having Finn around kept me energized—he certainly keeps me on my toes. I close my eyes.

My phone vibrates. It's my mother, but I only stare at the time. Nearly two hours have passed, but it feels like only a few minutes. I fall back asleep.

Somebody's car alarm goes off. I check my phone

again, hoping that Finn's name will be in one of the notifications—a text, a voice mail, even a missed call. No. But it's been five more hours. I feel like somebody must be playing a prank on me or I'm in Wonderland because there's no way that much time has passed. I lift my head off my pillow, feeling the slick heat of sweat. I pull the covers over my shoulder, a chill running down my spine.

I dream in bursts, my memory trying to compile them but only keeping fragments of each one. My mother is in one, presenting a giant box to me. In another, I'm surrounded by tiny horses with scorpion stingers. In one of them, I'm living in the 18th century, struggling to make enough money to eat. Finn is in every dream—he helps me open the box to reveal a puppy, he herds the tiny horse-scorpions into a corral, and he comes home riding a horse bareback. Absolutely nothing makes sense in these dreams, but every time I see him, the same rush of elation runs through me.

I wake up as my phone rings. My skin feels sticky with sweat. I fumble for the phone, grabbing it after the third ring.

"Hello?" I mumble.

"Hey, baby girl. I just got back this morning. I texted you, but you didn't answer, so I just wanted to be certain that you hadn't fallen and broken your hip or something."

"I'm not an old grandma."

"You sound like you could be one. Are you sick?"

I narrow my eyes. Ah. That would make the most sense.

"Wait. You said you got back this morning? What time is it?"

"It's nearly three."

"In the afternoon?"

"Yes," he pauses. "As tempted as I might be to call you at three in the morning, I wouldn't do that."

I rub my forehead. It's so grossly sweaty. "Crap. I've been sleeping for over twelve hours."

"Should I come over? Have you taken your temperature?"

"No." I try to sit up, but my body feels like I've done a million push-ups and at least twice as many sit-ups. My hair is sticking to my neck and I must smell worse than I look. "I'm, uh…is it okay if I just sleep through this? It's probably just a bad cold or something. It'll be over it soon."

"If that's what you want," he says, enough reluctance in his voice to make me doubt my own decision.

"We'll see each other soon," I promise.

"I'll see you soon then, baby girl."

"Yes, see you soon."

I let the phone fall from my hand. I start to close my eyes, sliding back down to a lying position but the need to be industrious pushes me onto my feet. Taking a shower will make me feel better.

I step into my bathroom. The world seems to become a kaleidoscope in front of my eyes and the last thing I remember is thinking that I need to put my hands out to save myself from hitting my head.

******

There are cool hands on my face.

Hmm. No. They're not cool. My body is just burning a hundred degrees. Or more.

I turn my head. Everything still looks a fuzzy and goes in and out of focus, but I can see Finn's blue eyes—like beacons, leading me home.

I cover my hands with my face, turning away from him. "Don't look. I'm gross."

He doesn't say anything. I feel his arms slip underneath me, picking me up as easily as if I weighed nothing. As I become more conscious, my organs begin to feel like they're burning. When Finn steps outside—carefully maneuvering me to open the doors—the cold breeze feels like Heaven, but my insides still feel like Hell. Finn sets me in the passenger seat of his car and I feel the seatbelt cross over my chest. My head lolls against the seat. I try to sit up—look at least a little presentable—but my body betrays me as it refuses to cooperate. I close my eyes.

When I open my eyes again, there's just a blur of

cars as Finn is speeding into a parking lot. The bright, glaring lights of the hospital make me think of lightning. Finn parks, then appears on my side of the car, unbuckling my seatbelt, and lifting me out.

Everything feels so strange. Maybe this is still a dream. Maybe a circus bear and a man with three eyes will appear soon. As long as Finn doesn't disappear, I'd be okay with it.

I'm sitting near a tall desk. Finn is talking to somebody—his voice urgent, angry, emphatic like the way he talks to people who think they have the upper hand over him, only to realize they're disposable.

That's my man. My daddy.

Daddy? I squint my eyes, staring down at my knees. It's a little weird, but it fits. Perfectly. He takes care of me, he protects me, he leads me, he provides for me, he disciplines me—my daddy.

I zone out as my mind tries out the word over and over. At first, I think I must be saying it aloud because Finn keeps glancing over at me as a nurse pushes me in a wheelchair down the hall, but I realize it's concern on his face—concern over my health. This is the way I've always wanted somebody to care for me, but now that I have it, it seems terrifying. After all, if I lose these feelings he has toward me, then it will be unequivocally my fault. I'll be the idiot who lost it all.

The nurse puts an IV in me as a way to keep me hydrated. It's hard to concentrate on her words, but Finn seems to be taking control and dealing with everything, so I'm not worried. I rest my head on the gurney pillow. I hope this isn't a dream. Despite this feeling of being weak, useless, and achy, it feels good to know that Finn would go through all these lengths for me. Someone who just wanted to fuck me wouldn't go through all this. At least, I don't think so.

I close my eyes and collapse into sleep.

******

I dream that I'm in the center of a forest fire. Trees and embers are falling all around me. I try to move, but my body is paralyzed. Every few minutes or seconds, maybe even hours, I feel myself starting to wake as I recognize I'm in a dream, but the dream sucks me back into it. I can't escape the idea that my own mind wants me to burn.

"I didn't take her to this hospital for her to be in stasis."

I hear Finn's voice. I try to follow it, knowing it could lead me out of this nightmare.

"Where is the doctor? Get him for me."

He's angry. I never hear or see him angry. In the chaotic *Torv Global* office, he's the one person I can always turn to in order to feel like everything is going to be okay. His leadership style is usually calm and in control.

My eyes open slowly. My eyelashes feel like they're glued together. I don't know how long I've been in this hospital, but all of the lights are dimmed and I don't see anybody familiar except for Finn.

It's a good thing he's attracted to me or else I would have died having to look at that face every day without being able to touch it, to feel his lips, to know that he hasn't let his good physique stop him from perfecting his technique.

As my thoughts about Finn wander, the piercing heat in my body becomes more apparent to me. The forest fire feels like it's in my chest and stomach. The ache under my skin has become more fierce like my muscles have spent days contracted.

"Mr. Garrett, I'm Dr. Albin. I heard that you had some concerns."

The doctor is out of my line of view, but he sounds like an older man.

"Sarah's temperature hasn't decreased. She's still grimacing while she's sleeping. She hasn't improved at all. The infection hasn't weakened."

"If the antibiotics don't work, we will try another method, but we can't overload her body with drugs. In my opinion—"

"Dr. Albin, let me see her chart."

"Mr. Garret, I assure you, we know what we're doing. If you could just—"

"Let me see the damn chart!"

I turn my head a little. Finn and Dr. Albin are standing an inch apart, staring at each other with enough tension in their eyes, it almost reminds me of my parents. The doctor slides the chart out from under his arm and holds it out to Finn. Finn takes it, his eyes scanning it the moment it's in front of him.

"This drug name on here and the drug in her IV aren't the same," he says. "How the hell does a hospital like this mess that up?"

Finn shoves the chart back to the doctor and he almost drops it. The doctor moves around Finn, giving him a wide berth. I hear him move near my bed. He mutters something under his breath.

"I'm sorry, Mr. Garrett," he says. I hear the shuffle of feet as the doctor moves back toward the door. "It must have been one of the nurses."

"I don't care who it was, but if this has any effect on Sarah's health, I will tear this hospital to the ground. Do you understand? Write that down on your chart."

"I'm sorry, Mr. Garrett," the doctor mumbled. "I'll go get the right antibiotics immediately."

There's a squeak as the doctor's shoes pivot. I hear Finn yank the curtain closed again. He sits back down beside me. His eyes light up as he realizes I'm awake. He leans close to me, kissing my cheek.

"How are you feeling baby girl?" he asks, taking my hand in his. His skin still feels cool compared to mine—opposite to the way it usually is—but it feels good.

"Never better," I mutter. He smiles because he thinks I'm joking, but it feels incomparably good to be cared for. I can't imagine that love is always like this— safe and reckless at the same time. It feels too intimate and when Finn squeezes my hand, I know that what I feel for him is unparalleled. Still, I pray for the miracle that he feels the same love. Maybe, just maybe, he does.

******

I wake in a cold sweat. I can't seem to catch my breath and the machine next to me is making a horrid noise.

Two nurses run up next to my bed. One of them yells toward the hall, "Yes sir." I then hear footsteps and see the doctor hurry next to me.

The stethoscope is cold on my chest. I hear them speak quickly as they each move around the room with such speed that my eyes dart to the next one moving and I can't figure out what is going on except that the air I'm breathing doesn't seem to be working. I can't get enough and I'm panting as though I'm in a dead sprint.

I hear part of a conversation but don't follow it except for the last sentence, "We've got to slow her heart rate down," which the doctor said angrily to the nurses. He then points a light in each of my eyes before quickly moving it away.

A nurse comes back and puts something into my I.V. The doctor then watches the monitor between looks back to his watch. The beeping sounds grow faster. Finally, the doctor actually speaks to me. "Sarah, you are having a severe reaction the antibiotic. We've given you medicine for that but you have to help us slow your heart rate. I want you to breathe slowly as I count." He begins to count and when he gets to five he says, "Now exhale." He counts to five again and says, "Inhale." I look around for Finn. He's gone. I try to focus on my breathing and on the doctor's voice. "Sarah, focus. You've got to stay with me." The beeping is still faster and another noise now accompanies it that I assume means things have gone from bad to worse as another nurse runs in. My hands begin shaking and jolting as though they are being pulled up and down by puppet strings.

The doctor stops speaking to me, apparently giving up on the breathing strategy. After opening a drawer but apparently not finding what he wanted, he steps into the hall and turns to his right to speak with someone just walking up. I hear pieces.

"Sir, no, I can't let you come in. It's critical and I need to get back."

The other person doesn't respond, I hear the footsteps sound over the scurrying of the nurses. The doctor follows, "Sir!"

I can't focus my eyes. It's all a foggy blur. I'm

dying. I'm about to pass out. I can't slow down. I can't catch up.

"Baby girl."

The voice sounds from my right and I turn, unable to focus my vision. That voice. I know that voice. I love that voice. It's so soothing.

The most recent sound that had been coming from the monitor stops. The beeping seems to be slower as all the medical people in the room position themselves around the machine.

"She's dropping!"

Three nurses and the doctor are staring at the monitor, but I can't take my eyes off the blurry spot I know to be Finn as my eyes slowly begin to regain the ability to focus.

"Normalizing!" one nurse says, in an are-you-kidding-me tone of voice, almost as though she's asking a question. All three turn back to me as the beeping continues to slow.

A few seconds pass before the nurse again speaks. "Normal."

Finn moves the same chair he had used before next to me and takes my hand. The doctor stares at Finn as though he's trying to solve a math problem before turning and walking out without a word.

I stare into Finn's eyes. He really is better than drugs. Dear God, please don't let that mean he is illegal.

******

"You tricked me into thinking you were a better man."

"I am a better man. Because of you. Because you believed in me."

"I don't believe you."

"But I love you and I will always love you. No matter what you say—"

"You are a liar! Go back to that whore from London."

My eyes snap open. It takes me a few seconds to realize the conversation is coming from a TV—the afternoon soap operas are on. I slept through the night and the next morning.

I touch my forehead. It's dry and only has a hint of the warmth it had last night. I raise my arms. They're a little achy, but nowhere near the pain I had been in last night.

I look to my left, where the chair is now. Finn isn't here. He must have gone back to work. I shouldn't have expected anything else, but it feels like a bit of my romantic fantasy has been shattered.

The sound of the soap opera stops. I listen to the beeps and low rumble of conversation in the hospital. Even surrounded by people, it feels a bit lonely and it's only made worse by the fact that there's still a needle in my hand, which leads to a tube that's connected to an IV pole. It's not like I can just walk out. One of these nurses will inevitably ask me where my dreamy, sweet boyfriend went and I'll have to tell them that he's just my boss.

The curtain slides open. When I see Finn, I'm overcome with a feeling of being completely healed. When I thought that modern medicine was a miracle, I hadn't taken into account the simple marvel of Finn's face.

Then, he smiles and all of my anxiety sheds away as well.

As he moves toward me and embraces me, I'm struck by the feeling that there is absolutely nobody else that I'd want to be stuck with in a hospital. If I could pick anybody, alive or dead, JFK or Mother Teresa wouldn't even be able to compete with Finn.

"How are you feeling?" he asks.

"Good." I grasp his arm, feeling the muscle flex underneath it. "I thought you had left."

His forehead wrinkles. "Why would I have left?"

"To go to work."

He shakes his head. "No, I just went to ask the lady next door to turn down the TV because you were sleeping. I wouldn't go to work while you were still here recovering."

"The company—"

"I've still been answering emails," he says, showing me his phone. "And coordinating everything that I can from here."

"You didn't need to stick around. I would have understood."

"I stuck around as much for you as I did for myself," he says. "I wanted to be certain that you kept improving. There was some time last night that I wasn't certain how this hospital trip would end."

My smile fades as I notice a vulnerability in his voice that I hadn't ever heard before. It's almost like a strain in his vocals, like he's been keeping back a million words or maybe that he's been whispering a million prayers.

He takes my hand, squeezing it. "I'm glad you're alright."

I wait for him to rush out, to say that now that I'm not minutes away from death, he has to go ensure that the office is doing everything in the way that he wants, but he sits down beside me and pulls the chair close. We talk about hospital food, the local news, and he even talks about how Marge came up with him as he climbed the ranks at Torv.

It feels like a real relationship and as I watch him—God, what a beautiful man—I can't help but entertain the idea that he loves me as much as I love him. I can almost taste this fantasy, feel it running in my bones, but I know I can't stay in this delusion too long. At some point, he'll get bored of me and all I'll be left with is this memory. All I can do is soak in all of it now and hope that I can pick myself up after this is done.

******

After the hospital releases me, Finn takes me back to my apartment. As he answers a business call, I check my own cell phone, which had been left here in the rush from the night before. There's a missed text from Erin, my mother, and three from Steve.

I click on the glowing "3" next to Steve's name.

How are you doing?

Sorry I was such an ass at your job

I was just joking around but I get why you'd be mad :)

Any interaction with Steve makes me wary, but it has been a couple years since we dated. Usually, when he did something that was wrong, he'd die before he admitted it. Maybe he's slowly maturing.

I text back.

It's okay.

I slide the phone back. As Finn walks back toward me, I try to look as sexy as a woman can look after spending a night in the hospital with a high fever.

"If I remember right, I made you pretty nervous at the hospital," I say. "That must make you a little mad."

"I'm certain your illness was punishment enough."

"I don't think so."

He raises an eyebrow, setting his phone on the

kitchen counter. I undo the button of my black pants, let them drop to the floor, and step out of them, moving closer to Finn. He watches me, his hand still hovering where he had left his phone. I strip off my blouse, leaving it right next to my pants. I move another step closer to him.

I had expected him to react faster than this. I hadn't seen him for a month, so I'm dying for his touch, but that doesn't mean he's dying for mine. He could have had a new woman in his bed every night in Paris. I reach toward him, my hand cupping his face.

"You know how I've been calling you *sir* and you call me *baby girl*?" I ask. He nods, his cheek rubbing against the inside of my palm. "Can I...can I call you Daddy?"

I flush, my gaze dropping toward my feet. He grabs me, spinning me around so quickly that I stretch out my arms to protect myself from any lack of balance. My hands end up on the edge of the kitchen counter. I feel his cock between my ass cheeks as he presses his body hard against me. His arm is wrapped around my waist, but his chest is pressed against my back, so I can't stand up straight. He sways against me and I can feel his arousal growing.

"I spent all that time worrying about you in the hospital and all you were thinking about was dirty names?" he whispers in my ear. I grip tighter onto the counter, trying to focus on playing along with this game when all I want to do is tear off my panties and feel him fuck me like he owns me.

"Yes," I breathe.

He jerks my panties down. "Well, now you're going to have to call me that until it's the only name you know."

"Okay, Daddy."

"Not yet," he says. "First, you need to stick that ass out farther."

He steps away from me. The absence of his heat is cruel, but the anticipation is growing in me like a rocket set to go off into the heavens. I take a few steps back, so my ass is jutting out. I lean against the counter to stop myself from falling.

The first spank is a lot harder than I expected. A small yelp escapes from my lips and my legs instinctively move away from him.

"Say it," he commands. My mind goes blank for a second. The second slap is just as hard as the first one, but it hits the exact same spot and my body jolts.

"Daddy," I say, the word rushing out. "Daddy!"

"I only said to say it once."

I shut my mouth. He smacks my ass again.

"Say it."

"Daddy."

His commanding presence radiates off him so strongly that even when there's that brief period when I feeling nothing—the split second numbness after his hand lashes against my ass—my body is tense as I anticipate the next flash of pain.

And I love it. Our secret art on my flesh, our understanding of how closely pain and pleasure are related, and the trust between us that builds with every mark he leaves on me. I've been entirely too reckless and careless with my actions in the past—the strange men, the drugs, walking around in bad neighborhoods without the slightest impulse of self-preservation—but with Finn I can explore all these sides of me that I've been too scared to show anybody else.

The next spank is enough to cause my knees to buckle. He catches me before I stumble. He spins me back around, so we're face-to-face. He kisses me hard enough that I'm certain every cell in his lips has left a mark on my mouth. The pattern of lines and shapes on my lips probably matches his now. When he lets me go, I slide down against the counter. He takes a few steps back and I watch him unbuckle his pants. It's hard to not move closer as he pulls his boxer briefs down and his erection is enough to remind me of every time he's fucked me before. The rush of anticipation is staggering.

I crawl toward him, my breasts swaying with every movement. As I move to kiss the head of his cock, I feel his fingers on my shoulder and he pushes me back.

"I didn't say you could touch me yet."

I can't help the small groan that comes out of my mouth.

"I want to see you play with yourself first. Sit here with your legs spread."

I sit, the tile on the floor feeling cold on my burning ass. I look straight at him as I rub my clit, our eyes focused together. It's honestly a pointless exercise—I haven't been able to get off without his cock inside me since the first time we had sex—but if it's what he wants, then I'm honored to do it.

"Lay on your back," he says. "And keep going."

I slide down onto the tile. I keep rubbing my clit, staring up at the ceiling. I hear Finn get on his knees between my legs. I rub harder.

When I feel his cock nudge against my hand, I pull my arm away, but he grabs my wrist before I can move my hand too far. He guides my hand to his cock, my wetness spreading across his skin. It takes all of my self-control not to move myself onto him. My pussy is throbbing and from the look in Finn's eyes, he knows it.

"Tell me what you want," he says.

"I want your cock."

"You have it," he says, indicating to my hand. "You're going to need to be a bit more specific. If you don't ask for what you need in life, you'll never get it."

"I want your cock inside me," I say, licking my lips. "I want your hands squeezing my ass where you spanked me as you fuck me. I want you to fuck me so hard that I won't be able to walk tomorrow."

He moves so fast that all I feel is his cock move

past my hand and the pressure of it against my pussy lips. I'm wet enough that there's minimal resistance, but as soon as he's inside me, I know he's going to fuck me as hard as I asked him to. I feel him push into me completely and it causes a full-body sensation that is fantastically familiar and foreign at the same time. Unlike most things in life, when he penetrates me, I'm struck by how it's even better than I remember. I didn't build it up in my mind. My memory couldn't do it justice. It's like a drug. My drug. And my escape from the known universe into one occupied only by this alpha man and me.

If I was in my right mind, I'd feel sorry for whoever lived in the apartment below me because it must sound like we're trying to demolish my kitchen. With one hand clawing into my right ass cheek and the other hand on my breast, he rams into me with enough reckless abandon that I can't imagine how good the sex will be when he's actually angry. Or maybe he is now— maybe all his pent-up concern is pouring out now as rage and nothing has gotten me hotter.

My back slides against the tile until my head is propped up against the kitchen cabinet.

He and I are in this place of condemnation because he's my boss. I would gladly burn on the stake for him, but I would never let him face the jeers of the crowd. Still, this is all I need. In these moments, he is all mine and he owns all of me.

He moves his hand right below my neck and for a second, I think he knows what I want. I can imagine the adrenaline as his fingers close around my throat and I could be his helpless baby girl.

But he keeps his hand where it is. I place my hand over his, trying to pull it up, but the first couple of times that I move his hand up, he slides it back down. The third time I drag it up, here keeps it there, but there's no pressure.

In the end, it doesn't matter. I can feel that urgency in my body about to reach its peak. My head involuntarily falls back and I buck against him as he thrusts into me. He wraps his arm around me, pulling me close to him. We kiss. I'm nearly ready to bite into his shoulder when the tidal wave of pleasure slams into me. Its force feels as though it's leaving and entering me at the same time as my entire body is rendered near paralytic.

My ears ring and my body jolts. Once it feels the air has gone from my lungs, I'm left as a trembling doll in his arms. He thrusts into me one more time, his body pressed tightly against mine as he exhales loudly and I feel his warm cum explode inside of me.

He slides down on the floor beside me, his breathing labored. As my heart rate slows, I turn on to my side. I lay my palm on his chest, enjoying the feeling of his heart beating under my hand. I lay my head on the side of his chest and rest with him.

These are the moments I live for: the chaos of the hurricane followed by the calm after the storm. Everything feels more peaceful after a war and all I want is to lie next to my victorious commander.

Chapter 12
CHAOS OF THE HURRICANE

Marge has an addiction to pistachios. She keeps a bag of them at the desk and there's a constant pile of shells in the trash can. I mentioned it to Finn once and he admitted to once buying her a barrel of pistachios because she liked them so much. I told him that I definitely liked hundred dollar bills more than Marge liked pistachios. He seemed to contemplate it, so I quickly said that I didn't want anything from him I hadn't earned. I'm still not completely certain I won't arrive at work to find a barrel of money.

It's lunch break, so I hear her munch on her pistachios as I check Tumblr. It's a bad habit I had started in college—I just check in every few days, reblogging quotes I like, photography posts, and posts made by authors I like. Through my harder days, it made me feel like I was living a life where other people understood how I felt and I could pretend I was standing in front of a beautiful, but rugged landscape.

"Do you want some pistachios?" Marge asks me. I

shake my head. I hear the elevator beep and the doors open. I look over my shoulder just as Finn steps into the room. At the same time, my phone vibrates. I check it. It's Steve again. He's been consistent with his texts since I replied to him—his questions lingering on the line between intrusive and casual.

What did you do tonight?

Are you hanging out with anyone this weekend?

Do you still live alone?

Today, it just says: *Can we meet for lunch? I left my briefcase at your place a while ago and you know how much it means to me...*

As Finn passes by the desk, I remember that one of the board members had called.

"Daddy—"

I stop, my cheeks burning hot so fast that it reminds me of how my ass looks when he spanks it. It was a slip of the tongue, but I can feel Marge's eyes burning into the back of my head.

Think, Sarah, think. There has to be a way to make this look normal.

"Uh...my daddy called," I say. "I...just wanted to tell you because...it's his birthday."

Finn looks like he's about to burst out laughing, the sides of his eyes drinking and the corner of his mouth curving up.

"Oh?" he asks. "Are you going to give your Daddy a present?"

I scowl at him. "I will figure out what to give him soon."

"Well, if his birthday is today, you're running out of time."

I hear the single crack of a pistachio shell being broken apart, but I can still feel Marge's eyes on us. "I'll just have to get him a gift card then."

"I don't think that's what most men want. Did you want to tell me anything else other than the fact that your Daddy called?"

"Uh, yeah. One of the board members called." I check my note. "It was Jared Wright. He needs you to call him back as soon as possible he said."

Finn nods. "Thank you. I'll call him back and maybe after we can figure out what to give your Daddy."

He glances at my laptop as he passes by. As soon as he's locked himself in his office, I turn back to Tumblr, pretending to be immersed in its content. Marge clears her throat. In my periphery, I see her mouth open, then close again. I turn to her, feeling a lot braver after seeing how closely Finn toed the line.

"What?" I ask.

"I bet your father would like jerky," she says. "Men love jerky."

"Thanks," I say. I turn back to my laptop. This could not be any more embarrassing. Marge has to be at least a little suspicious.

I hear the office door unlock and Finn pops his head out.

"Marge, could you pick up Jared at the airport? I'd send Sarah, but you know how Jared is."

"He does love women a couple decades younger than him. What time does the plane land, Mr. Garrett?"

"In about half an hour, so you should go now. After you've done that, you can go home," Finn says. "Sarah can finish up here."

"Thank you, Mr. Garrett."

As Marge shuffles toward the elevator, Finn smirks at me.

"Stop," I say. "It's how I think of you now. It's not my fault that it slipped out."

"It's definitely your fault," he says. "And I wish I had time to punish you."

His hand brushes against mine as he reaches toward the desk. He takes a sheet of paper off of it, but it only brings my attention back to my phone.

"My ex, the guy who was here, he wants to see me for lunch," I say. Finn nods, reading the paper. It's just a letter from one of the foundations that the company gives to, thanking us for our donation. I continue. "He left his briefcase at my apartment years ago. I would have given it away, but it has his father's initials in it who died when he was young, so…that's also why he wants it back. I haven't said if I'd go yet. I'll call it off completely if you want me to and just get it to him another way."

Finn glances up from the paper. "I'll understand either way. You can do what you want."

This isn't the response I wanted, but it should have been the response I expected. He has no reason to be jealous of me meeting with my ex.

I grab my phone. As I unlock the screen, Finn grabs my wrist. He looks straight at me.

"I'd rather you call it off. I know I don't know him, but something doesn't feel right about him. Just a gut feeling."

"Okay," I say, though I'm smiling so broadly that it hurts my face. After he sets the paper back down, two of his fingers brush against the pulse in my wrist.

Every place he touches me is a place where hope grows and I can't wait until all of our hopes are fulfilled.

******

Why can't we meet for lunch?
I don't want to meet with Erin.
I thought you were more mature than this Sarah.

My cell phone starts ringing after the barrage of tweets from Steve. I don't look at it. There's a love song playing on the radio that makes me think of Finn—or not Finn exactly, but who I imagine I could be with Finn or who he could be if I was somebody more meaningful to him. It's Friday night and everyone else seems to be out with their loved ones except me. And Steve, apparently.

As I sit in my bedroom, the simple instrumentation of the piano begins to fade away as the singer's voice whispers about being trapped in a never-ending dance. My phone has stopped ringing, but it immediately starts again as Steve tries to get through to me. I knew he would call again. As much as an asshole Steve was, there was some comfort to our relationship—I knew what made him happy, what still makes him angry, and I know what to expect out of our relationship.

I know some things that make Finn happy and angry, but I can't have any expectations about our future. It's the one major flaw in our relationship—it has to remain secret and I'm too afraid of losing it to question any of it. Steve and I could show our relationship status on Facebook. We could sleep at each other's places. I wouldn't have to share him with French models and whoever the hell else he hooks up with when he's gone or going to banquets. The chaos during sex is thrilling, but in everyday life, it would be nice if I could be more than an office whore to him. Surely I am.

I pick up my phone.

"Hello?" I answer.

"What were you doing? I've been texting and calling you. You could have been murdered for all I know."

"Sorry, I had turned my phone to silent after my lunch break. I forgot to turn it back on," I say. "You know how I am…"

"Well, I thought you would have improved a bit by now," he says. He clears his throat. "Which leads us back to the fact that you think you can't meet me just to give me back my bag."

"I'm….I'm seeing someone right now," I say. "And he doesn't like the idea of me meeting with you."

"What? What the hell? Why didn't you mention this before? Who the hell is he? Who the hell are you seeing?"

"I don't think that's any of your business—"

"Damn, you're so immature. Why wouldn't you tell me? What do you think I'm going to do? Beat up the guy? Let's be honest: the only reason you didn't tell me is because you still have feelings for me. You didn't want to risk the chance that I'd become disinterested if I found out you were dating someone else. So, if you—"

"That's not what's going on at all."

"You need to tell me who it is."

"Why does it even matter?"

"Because you are a terrible judge of character."

There's an edge of malice in his tone, but he's also right with his last statement. The fact that he knows me so well is unnerving.

"I don't think—" I start.

"Sarah."

"—he's a bad guy."

"Sarah. Don't be a bitch about this. It's a simple question. What's the big deal?"

"I just don't think you need to know."

"You're acting like I'm asking you to move mountains or get me a date with Angelina Jolie. I just want to know who you're dating. Sarah, for God's sake, you should hear yourself sometimes. Nothing is that special in your life that you need to keep it a secret."

His voice is like a tick, burrowing under my skin and sucking out any resistance I have. It's late. This conversation is absurd.

"It's my boss," I blurt. "Okay? It's no big deal. It's not serious."

There's silence on the other end of the phone and, as someone who knows Steve as well as he knows me, I know it's incredibly rare for him to be speechless. I wait for him to say something, my fingers drumming against my nightstand.

"Are you shitting me?" he finally asks. "Your boss? You're screwing your boss? That pretentious dick who kicked me out of the *Torv Global* building?"

"He thought you were bothering me."

"No, he just wanted to throw his dick around. Shit! You really can't be trusted to do anything, can you? Dating your boss. What in God's name compelled you to do something so stupid?"

"It was just a thing that happened. I—"

"You need to break it off with him," he cuts me off. "You clearly can't be trusted to make these kinds of decisions. Just move back in with me. I'll get you back on the right path. We're both about ten or fifteen years older than you so you still get that. You were better with me."

"No," I say. "I wasn't better with you."

"Sarah," he growls. "Don't be so naive. This guy will date you and dump you as soon as he's bored. That's what these pretentious guys do. Why do you think he's dating you? I'm sure he has women falling all over him, but if he fucks you in secret, he can fuck other women without them being concerned that he's fucking you. It's a brilliant plan. I'll applaud him for that. But don't be so stupid to fall for it. We both know that you don't offer enough to be any more than a quick piece of ass to him."

"I think this conversation is over."

"Sarah—"

I hang up. After a few seconds, my cell phone starts ringing again. I wish I could say I hung up on him because I knew he was wrong, but I fear that the real reason is because I know he's right. He just voiced all my deepest fears and I barely had to tell him anything.

I turn my phone to silent. I get into my bed, still dressed in my work clothes, and turn off the lamp on my nightstand.

I wish I was strong enough to tell Finn that I can't

be with him anymore because I hate being a secret, but it's just another time that I'm too weak to quit what I'm addicted to.

******

When Finn told me he was taking me to *Niccolò's Colosseum*, there was a part of me hoping that he was taking me here to tell me he was going to make our relationship public, but the more I thought about it, the more I knew it wouldn't happen. The Board of Directors would fire him immediately for fear that the public would see it as an abuse of power. It was a five-second fantasy and nothing more, but as I sit across from him now in the place that we had our first date, I'm overwhelmed with the feeling of gratitude. I may love this man more than he will ever love me, but just to be in his presence is enough for me. For now.

"What are you thinking?" he asks, gesturing to the menu in front of me, which I never picked up. "The same thing you had last time? A medium Delmonico ribeye?"

"I think you should order for me," I say. "I trust Daddy's judgment over mine."

He smirks but doesn't say anything else as he reads the menu.

"There's something else I want to try too," I say.

"You're feeling pretty adventurous tonight."

I lean forward, so I don't have to talk as loud. "I've had this fantasy for a while."

He peers over his menu, a strong sliver of interest in his eyes. "Go on."

"I want to be choked."

The sliver in his eyes shifts to uncertainty and he looks back down at the menu. "Well."

I clench my fists under my chest as I lean farther over the table. "It's not that different from spanking."

"Your life is never at risk when I'm turning your ass red."

"I trust that you would know when to stop."

He takes a deep breath. "I see."

"Are you saying that I shouldn't trust you?"

He looks back up at me and sets down the menu. "Sarah…if you want to do it, we can try it, but you need to stop me as soon as you think it's gone too far. There can't be any hesitation on your part."

The flutter of happiness at his relenting is slightly dampened by the realization that he never answered my question about trusting him.

"Good," I say, sitting up straight again. "We should try it tonight."

"You're getting a little demanding, aren't you?" he asks, taking my menu from in front of me. "We may have to deal with that before I give you anything else."

"That's a long time to wait for a punishment," I say.

"I'll make sure it's good enough that you remember it for a long time."

Our waiter, Joseph, returns to our table. "Sir, ma'am, are you ready to order?"

"She's going to have the Delmonico ribeye, medium. I'll have the porterhouse, medium-rare," Finn says.

"Thank you, Daddy," I say to Finn. The waiter glances between us, a little confused, but Finn just smiles casually.

"Thank you, Joseph. That's going to be it for us."

"Of course, sir. Thank you, sir." Joseph does something like a small bow, sneaking a quick peek at me with a more mischievous look on his face before striding away. I'm certain he's going to go tell everyone that works here what just happened. It's both mortifying and electrifying.

That man has that young woman calling him Daddy!

Yes, yes, he does. He has complete power over me and there's no place I'd rather be than under him.

"That was interesting," Finn says, taking my hand and squeezing it.

"You didn't like it?"

"I thought it was great," he says, grinning. "You may end up getting that punishment early. We might have to get in the back of my Benz again in a parking lot close by. I bet there's enough room there for me to drag my cock all over that pretty face."

I shift my weight. I can't let him make me too wet when I'm wearing this thin of a dress.

"I'm sure there is," I say. "But that wouldn't be a punishment for me."

He continues to gaze at my face. I know he's imagining his cock on it—maybe with me lying down and him moving it across my nose or my tongue chasing it—because I'm imagining the same thing.

I'm just also imagining his hands around my neck, the lack of oxygen in my lungs, and to know that he has complete control over my literal existence.

My cell phone rings, clattering against something in my purse. I ignore it. I had Steve's number blocked from my cell, but he's already called me once from his job and I have no interest in talking to anyone but Finn right now.

"Come sit closer by me," he says. I slide around the booth to his side of the table. It's times like now when I wonder how far I'd be willing to go to chase this thrill. How explicit would I allow this discussion to get? Would I enjoy getting fucked in this restaurant's fancy bathroom? Would I blow him under this table?

I'm not sure I could deny him anything. It'd be denying myself. And part of the thrill is putting myself at the mercy of his command. It's an odd balance within me of trusting him not to go too far, but accepting it if he does.

Under the table, his hand rests on my knee. It creeps up my thigh, pushing the dress up. I feel the tingle between my legs and lean against his arm, trying to keep my breathing steady as my dress slowly gets pushed up to my hip and his fingers brush against the front of my panties. I squirm, his touch and his shamelessness instantly drawing wetness.

His fingers continue to pet me. It takes all of my self-restraint not to beg him to take me to his car and have his way with me, but he already said I was getting demanding, so I stay quiet. He reads the wine list while I pretend to concentrate on the flickering candle.

The waiter returns with two salads in his hand. By now, my cheeks are flushed and I suspect I looked a bit lightheaded. The waiter sets the salads in front of Finn but hesitates with mine.

"You can set Sarah's salad over there," Finn says, indicating to the side of the table where I had been sitting with his unoccupied hand. The waiter smiles, setting it down where Finn indicated.

"Enjoy your salads," he says, his eyes focusing on me for a second too long before slipping away. Finn stops touching me, gesturing to the other side of the table.

"Let's eat," he says.

It's…disappointing, to say the least. I'm aroused enough that any surface looks good enough to rub against, but I slide back across the booth to my side of the table. This may be the cruelest thing he has ever done in his life and yet everything that he does to me is the most genuine kindness.

And I can't wait to see what else he has up his sleeve.

Chapter 13
IF ONLY

This could be the last time.

The thought keeps intruding into my mind. As I lie on my bed, Finn joins me. His hands are an antidote to the nausea over the intrusive thought, but it still lingers.

I wish he'd tell me what to think, so my thoughts wouldn't be so uncertain and untrustworthy.

He had driven by the parking lot we had hooked up at last time, but somebody's car was already there, so he drove me to my apartment. I wasn't certain if he was giving up on our plans, so I was pleased when he followed me up to my place.

As we kiss, I can taste the bourbon, both sweet and smoky, that he'd been drinking and I try to remember every bit of it. His hands cup my face, then move up to my hair, tugging on the strands as his mouth presses against my throat. I close my eyes.

This could be the last time.

He stops, pulling away from me. "You're distracted."

"What? I don't think so. Am I?" I ask.

"You are," he says. "Is something going on?"

I shake my head. "No. Everything's fine."

He stares straight at me, his blue eyes vibrant even in the faint glow of the lamp in my bedroom. To prove my devotion to him and this moment, I unzip my dress, wiggling out of it slowly. As I undo his pants, I can feel all my concerns slipping away. This is what I love about being with him—it's so easy to forget that anybody else exists in the world and all these times that I should feel cautious or scared become moments that I trust him implicitly. He has never failed to make everything better.

After his pants are off, he indicates for me to lie back down on the bed. I lie on my back, staring up at the ceiling. He moves over me, his knees on either side of my chest. His cock—only semi-hard—slaps down on my cheek, the head of it nearly prodding my eye. The tip of my tongue barely touches it and I'm certain he knows that he's denying me what I want.

He moves his cock farther to the right, rolling over and squishing one of my nostrils. He pushes it down to my lips. I kiss the head of it and slip my tongue out to give it a crown of saliva.

"Baby girl."

He moves over my arms, so he can straddle my head. He rests his balls on my lips as the saliva-covered head of his cock teases my hairline. I open my mouth, taking part of his balls inside, my tongue twisting around them. All I want to do is please him and have him be pleased with me.

"Baby girl, there's so much I want to do to you. I'm going to hold you down and fuck you until you beg me to stop."

I'll never ask him to stop.

He moves his cock back to my mouth, rising up, so the tip of it slides into my mouth. I open my jaw as wide as I can and stick out my tongue. He rolls his swelling erection over my tongue, coating it completely before rubbing it over my lips like lipstick.

He raises a knee, swinging his body away from me. The sudden lack of warmth is jarring.

"Get on your hands and knees."

I do as he says, fast enough that the whole bed jiggles from my movement. He smacks me so hard on my ass that I fall on my face. The blanket gives me a soft landing, but there's a sudden contrast as Finn spanks my bottom hard three times in quick succession. I make small grunting noises as the air in my lungs is expelled.

"Did you think you were in control of this relationship?" he asks. "If I want to choke you, I'll choke you when I want to choke you. Do you understand?"

"Yes Daddy," I say, raising my backside up, hoping for more despite the radiating pain. Or maybe because of it. Three more whacks rain down on my bare ass. I can feel the warmth of tears threatening to come down. This pain is so much like sex—the pent-up tension from everyday life, released by my Daddy, giving me all his passion until we're both burnt out.

The last spank knocks me flat on the bed. He grabs me on the shoulders, flipping me over. As he kisses me, I feel that hint of a question, asking me if he's gone too far and I answer with kisses that border between submissive and egging him on. He gets off the bed. Before I can look up, he grabs me by the ankles, dragging me to the edge of the bed until my burning ass is almost dangling off it. He pushes my legs up toward my chest and I feel his cock at my entrance.

He thrusts into me with the same force as his spanking, but I'm so wet that there's only slight pain from the friction, and it's the good kind. He drives into me so hard that I can feel his balls slap against my ass. When I try to reach toward him, he grabs onto my wrists, pinning them down.

He knows my body so well that he knows the exact rhythm to drive me to the edge, then leave me needy and desperate as he slows down his pace. There is no greater torture than being so close to something you want and not being able to have it.

My thighs hit against my chest with every thrust. There's enough force that I won't be surprised if tomorrow I have a faint mark left and I can't wait to see it. Just another souvenir of something that won't last.

My thoughts are cut short as I feel his right hand leave my wrist and settle over my neck. He wraps his fingers around my throat—a reminder of how large his hands are and how easily he could raise or ruin me. He holds his hand there, his movements slowing down.

"I love…this," he says. The slight hesitation between his words is enough to make my heart beat much faster, but it beats even more rapidly as he applies pressure on my throat. I feel my body start to rebel, but the panic is dulled by the pure luxury caused by his cock.

He relaxes his hand just as my body starts to squirm. After a minute, he squeezes again. Adrenaline surges through me. I can feel my body starting to fight again, but I rise above it and put my mind over the matter. I embrace it. As my left hand reaches up to his face, he releases my neck and pins my hand down again. The adrenaline doesn't stop as he grabs onto my hips, returning to his rapid thrusts.

My heart is beating so hard that I feel like it could burst. I grip onto the blankets that have already been ripped away from the mattress, breathless mewling noises slipping out of me until an earthquake of pleasure sends shock waves of endorphins through me and my pussy clinches onto Finn's cock eagerly. I feel him cum inside me as I'm still in the eruption of an orgasm, the sound of his grunts and the warmth spreading inside of me extending the length and intensity of the wave.

I barely notice as he collapses down beside me. It takes several minutes for me to catch my breath. He strokes my neck, his fingers tracing where his hand had been and then wandering down to my clavicle.

"Thank you," I say. He laughs.

"That's a response I haven't heard before."

"Well, I mean it. And I'd like to be unique in your mind," I say, gingerly moving onto my side to look at him. He looks even sexier with a veneer of sweat on his body. He looks back at me. I can't quite read his face, but there's some flicker of an emotion in his eyes I haven't seen before. He sits up.

"It's late," he says. "I should get going."

The thought hits me again: *There is no greater torture than being so close to something you want and not being able to have it.*

"Of course," I say. "I'm sorry to keep you here."

He smiles at me. It's not quite pity on his face, but it's close enough to it that it's all I can see. "You don't need to apologize for anything."

He kisses my cheek, then my mouth. I watch him get dressed, locking my eyes onto his crotch to possess every second until he zips it hidden.

"I'll see you at work tomorrow."

"I'll be there."

After he leaves, I pick up my phone. One missed call from Steve's work number. By his standards, even he's giving up on me.

Being with Finn is a lot like cocaine. When I'm with him, it's the highest of highs, but when his presence has worn off, I'm farther down than I've ever been. If I could get him to stay, it would be a whole other story, but he won't ever stay. I'm just going to continuously watch him leave until he decides I'm no longer worth it. And that moment will shatter me.

******

When I wake up, my body feels like I stumbled down every step in *Torv Global*. I look in the mirror. My ass is a collage of blues and purples while there are small round marks on my chest from my knees hitting it as Finn fucked me. Liquid warmth flows through me just thinking about it now.

My whole body jerks as somebody knocks on the door. I grab a hoodie, zipping it up, and a pair of sweatpants. I hustle to the door, reminding myself that Finn just left last night and he wouldn't come around this early. Still, I smooth my hair and pray my breath doesn't smell terrible. I open the door.

It's Steve.

"What are you doing here?" I ask.

"Good morning to you too. Your hair's a mess."

He grabs me by the shoulders, abruptly moving me to the side. He's wearing cargo pants, which is strange since he has always worn jeans or dress pants. Maybe I'm lucky and he's met a woman who can actually change him, even if it's for uglier clothing.

"I thought we could talk," he says. I close the door, feeling my shoulders slump a little. I'm too tired to fight with him. I feel like even after I left him, the memory of him has worn me down until all that's left of my resistance is the firm conviction that I will never get back together with him.

"What do you want to talk about?"

"You dating your boss. Mr. Finn Garrett."

"What about it?"

"Well, how exactly does it work? Does he drive you home? Does he give you bonuses when he fucks you?"

"If you're going to be rude, you can leave."

"These aren't hard questions," he says. "Unless the answer is yes and you're ashamed."

"I'm not ashamed."

"Then, tell me. What happens between you two?"

I sigh, crossing my arms over my chest. "We have dinner together sometimes. We talk."

"You have sex," he presses. His attitude is confusing. Maybe he is changing because usually the mere thought of me having a sex with another man would send him into a rage-fueled tailspin, but he seems eager now to hear the details.

"Yeah. That happens sometimes," I say. I wait for

him to lash out, but he just nods several times and touches his greasy hair like he's checking to see if it's still there.

"So, you'd say you're in a sexual relationship with Finn Garrett?"

"I don't know if I'd definitely call it a relationship, but sure, it could be called that."

He lifts up the pocket flaps of his cargo pants. He pulls out his cell phone. He shows it to me. It has a large red recording button and 00:41:03 on the screen.

"What is that?" I ask. He taps on the screen twice. There's a rustling sound for several seconds and then I hear my voice after four seconds.

"What are you doing here?"

"Good morning to you too. Your hair's a mess."

I stare at him. "You recorded our conversation?"

"Well, see, I know how these big businesses work. The slightest embarrassment will force the board of directors to do whatever they can to fix the problem. Didn't *Torv Global* just have a scandal with that anti-Semitic model? And you know what scandal those board of directors are most afraid of? Sexual assault allegations."

"Nobody sexually assaulted anybody!"

"No, not legally, but the board won't care about that. They'll care how it looks though if their top man is screwing his assistant. You could claim everything was consensual, but the board would say there was no way you could consent when he had so much power over you. They would be wary that you would change your mind and claim things weren't consensual. They can't risk that. They'd fire your boss and he'd end up having to work at a fast food restaurant because no other company would risk their reputation taking him on at even an entry-level position."

I grab his arm. "You can't tell them!"

"Why wouldn't I?" he asks. "I have no reason not to."

I release his arm. "Because I don't want you to."

"Why would I care what you want? You don't care what I want."

"I do care what you want. If you want money, a job, a therapist—"

"I want you to realize we were always meant to be together."

"I don't want to be with you."

He taps on his cell phone screen.

"I thought we could talk."

"What do you want to talk about?"

"You dating your boss. Mr. Finn Garrett."

He presses on the screen again and the recording goes silent.

"Are you really trying to blackmail me?" I ask.

"You know, blackmail only works on people doing something bad."

"We're not doing anything bad."

"Fine, I'll just take this to the board. Jared Wright is one of the board members, right? My cousin is a member at the same country club as him."

He turns to the door. I put my hand on his shoulder.

"Please give me some time to think about it."

He considers me, his eyes lingering on my cleavage. I zip my hoodie up higher. "You have until the end of the day."

******

I sit behind Finn in the conference room as he talks to members of the *Torv Global Foundation*. I type up notes about their plans to fund after-school activities for schools that can't afford it in the city. Finn is as commanding as ever, steering the conversation in whichever way it needs to go without any of the other members noticing how firmly he has a grip on the discussion.

There's an ache deep in my chest knowing how much he loves his work and how good at it he is. He needs it. If I cause him to lose this job, it will mean I ruined his life.

I save the document to the tablet as the meeting ends and the six members of the foundation shake Finn's hand as they leave. I'm about to follow them out when Finn touches the inside of my wrist.

"Can we talk for a second?" he asks, indicating to his office. This would normally thrill me, but I know any chance I get to talk to him alone should be a time when I tell him about Steve. But I can't risk telling him about Steve because it will put pressure on him to deal with this dilemma. Steve is my problem. Finn didn't do anything to cause this.

After he closes the door to his office, I sit down in the chair across from his desk. He leans against his desk in front of me. I can imagine every inch of his body under his suit and I just want to feel it pressed up against me. I want to feel the callouses on his hands caused by him spanking me. I had thought so often about him leaving his mark on me, it had never occurred to me that I had done the same to him.

We can do it one last time and I can pretend it's just like the first time.

"Is everything okay with you?" he asks, "You've barely said a word all day."

"I've been busy."

"You've been far busier on other days than today. Raise your head up."

I lift my chin up a little, trying not to think because I'm convinced he can read my mind.

"More than that. I want to see your neck."

"Oh." I look up at the ceiling, showing him my throat. "It's fine."

"Are you burnt out? Do you need a few days off?"

I shake my head. "I just need...some pain. Some punishment."

The edge of his lips curves up. "Am I your pain dealer?"

"What can I say? You have me addicted." I slide off the chair onto my knees. I curl a finger through one of his belt loops. "I'll do anything for it."

"You know I'd love to, but I have another meeting in less than fifteen minutes and the way we do things, it's never less than half an hour."

I grab onto his hand swinging it back and forth like a small child. "Please, Daddy?"

He sighs. "Get your pants off, baby girl."

I leap to my feet, undoing my pants as quickly as I can and pushing them down. As I start to pull my panties down, he grabs me, causing me to trip in my pants. I manage to get them off my ankles as his fingers grip my thin panties, tearing them down the middle. The pieces fall between my legs.

"Get on your hands and knees on the desk."

I clamber onto his desk. As I settle on my hands and knees, I find myself staring at a magazine cover with Finn Garret's name on it. *The Torv Global CEO's secret to success!*

I suppose it would be a more tantalizing headline if it said: *The Torv Global CEO's secret to demise! A downfall caused by his assistant.*

When nothing happens, I turn around to look at

Finn. At the exact same moment, his hand comes down, hitting the center of a bruise I had highly admired for its perfect circular shape. It sends a shock through my body. I can't be certain if he was holding out during our first couple of sessions, but he seems to have perfected his spanking on me. The strength of the blows change—first hard, then so soft they could barely be considered slaps, but then there are a few blows that nearly cause me to fall flat on my stomach. I bite my lip every time, unladylike grunts coming from my throat as I try to remain quiet. I wouldn't be surprised if Finn had made his office soundproof for this kind of thing—I'd never heard a single sound when I work right outside his door.

The heat from my ass seems to seep straight through my skin and bloom in my pussy. I'm already getting wet enough that I can feel my arousal cooling on my leg. As I reach toward my pussy, Finn hits me twice as hard. My breasts sway with every hit and I can feel his eyes fixate on them. Just the thought of turning him on is enough for me and as the next smack causes my legs to buckle, I rub up against the wood of his desk, which is more mortifying than anything else, but I can't help myself.

He grabs me around the waist, spinning me around. My back hits the desk hard, but I don't have time to think about it as his hand—the one he must have spanked me with since it's so warm—covers my pussy. His fingers slide inside me and I buck against his touch.

Each one of his fingers are experts as the heel of his palm rubs against my clit and his curved fingers move in and out of me. I arch my back as his fingers find all the right places.

I can barely suppress a whimper as he removes his hand. He unbuttons his shirt while I watch him. Every smooth movement of his fingers feels like a seduction. I wouldn't mind being so casually thrown to the side like he does with his shirt as long as he eventually lies down beside me.

I wait for him to climb onto the desk with me, but he's drawing out this torture. He takes off his watch while I slide closer to the edge of the desk, hoping to convince him not to make me wait any longer. He glances up at me. I smile at him, the hazy, needy feeling of arousal coursing through me, making me feel both invincible and vulnerable. It's a smile I could only give to a man that owned me completely.

He takes my hand, his thumb brushing against my skin as he wraps the watch around my wrist and fastens it. When he lets go, it slides partway down my arm.

"Turn around and keep your eyes on that second hand. When it's been a minute, you can turn around."

I spin around on the desk, the pulse between my legs feeling like a ticking bomb. I stare at his watch, a bit unnerved by the various hands on it. I focus on the large one, waiting as it seems to move as slowly as possible. I swear it jerks back a little every few seconds.

When the minute ends, I spin back around. Finn is naked, his cock making the ticking bomb between my legs beat even faster. I move toward him like I'm in a dream. My body feels like it's floating as I get off the desk. I reach toward him, my hands on his face as I kiss him. How could I ever give this up? How could I live without the combative way he kisses and without that finger he knows how to twist me around?

As we kiss, he grabs onto my thigh, jerking half my body up. As he grabs onto my other leg, I lean slightly away from him, feeling for his cock with one hand while my other arm wraps around his neck. I aim his cock at my entrance and he jerks his hips forward. His immensity feels like it fills me, but I feel his fingertips dig into my thighs and he pushes into me farther.

It starts out slow. He rocks his body back and forth like we're on a ship and he's creating the waves. I look into his eyes and see the most beautiful oceans, reminding me of the existence of a freedom I can only ever briefly experience with him. It's so nice to let go of all thought, all decisions, and all memories and just have him tell me exactly what I should be doing and knowing he will always fulfill me. In this moment, that's enough.

He breaks our trance, his gaze shifting to my breasts. He bends his head down, flicking his tongue over my right nipple. It sends electricity straight down to my pussy. He blows on it, causing a chill to follow the electricity. He does the same to the other nipple. I buck against him, my body ready to set itself on fire and enjoy the ignition.

My nails dig into his shoulder as he pushes me up against the southern brick wall of his office. He's barely holding onto my thighs, but there's never a second that I'm afraid of falling. There's no space for fear, only my body recognizing his body as the perfect drug and I'll take hit after hit after hit of it until I'm completely satisfied.

I brush my lips against his cheek, our movements too frantic to have any precision. I can feel the thickness of his cock inside of me, smell the scent of his sweat, wrap myself in the warmth of his skin, and enjoy every part of his body that touches mine with the same intensity. I know I'll be just another fuck, long forgotten in a couple of weeks, but I'll remember this forever.

The tension is reaching its peak and I can feel my body about to derail from composure. I try to push back faster against him, but he has complete control.

As I begin to feel frustrated for the first time over his authority of me, he jackhammers into me. I feel that pressure break, a flood drowning out any negative feelings, causing such a wreck in me that I fling my arms against the wall and I can imagine how sacrilegious I look. I feel my pussy rapidly pulsing around his cock. He thrusts into me once more, pinning me against the wall as he comes inside me. I feel the familiar, but always even-better-than-I-remember sensation of his warmth surging inside of my body.

He lowers me down slowly to the wooden floor, keeping a hold of me as we both lie down. I feel so good, so amazingly cherished, that I try to keep my mind on this moment. I don't want to think about anyone else but Finn. I don't want any time span to exist except the ones when we're this close together.

He sits up slowly. "I think I'm late for that meeting. I'll have to tell them there was traffic."

I get up, thinking about my phone to check the time, but I remember I'm still wearing his watch. I look down at it and the air leaves my lungs.

"I—I'm sorry," I say. I rub the glass of the watch. "Oh my God. I can't believe…you can take the money out of my salary. I'll…I can sell something from my apartment."

"What is it?" he asks. I fumble to get his watch off.

"I'm sorry," I say. "I'm so, so sorry. I should have taken it off. It was while we were…it was just now…I just lost control. I didn't mean to…they can replace the glass right?" I hold my hands over my mouth as I watch his reaction.

He takes the watch from me, where three deep scratches from the brick wall are evident. For the first time, I don't want him to be angry enough to punish me, though I'm willing to take whatever he deems best. If he decides I'm no longer worthy of his time in any form, I'd understand. I'm certain the watch is worth more than my life.

"It's fine," he says. He slips the watch into his pants pocket, then pulls the pants on. "Don't worry about it."

"No, no. I have to pay you back for it."

"I was the one who put it on you. I should have remembered your habit of interpretive dance during sex."

I chuckle, relieved that he doesn't seems angry. "I do not do interpretive dance during sex."

He shakes his head, a tiny smile on his face. "It's just good to know you enjoyed it that much."

"I'll find a way to pay you back for it."

"And I'll reject it," he says. He's already buttoning his shirt. "I have to go now to get to the meeting in time. I'll be back before you leave since we need to talk about how to get the *Luminary Foundation* to work with us."

"I'll be waiting," I say, pulling on my pants. I hear him close the door as I yank on my blouse. I'll have to tell him tonight. I'm running out of time.

Chapter 14
DUMPING MR. DARCY

Luminary Foundation spends an inordinate amount of its money on its products, but it's one of the biggest nonprofit organizations in NYC. They focus on providing education for as many people as possible, but convincing them to give up some of their funds to a corporation in order to create a new charity is going to be difficult. The only possible reason they would agree is if we could bring in more money for them and convince them that it isn't just an attempt to save face after the controversy with Kate Andrés.

I hear the elevator doors open, but I keep my head down. I know it's Finn as his hand rests on my shoulder. The familiarity and the warmth would normally be a comfort, but it feels like a final gesture I'll remember decades from now when I reflect on our relationship.

I turn toward him. "How was the meeting?"

"Long, but eventually productive." He indicates to his office. "Let's go talk."

"I don't think we should," I say. "We don't end up

doing a lot of talking in there."

"I wasn't aware you had any issues with our lack of conversation."

"I didn't. I don't. But..." I take a deep breath, holding it in for a few seconds before letting it out.

"Sarah, I'm not angry about the watch. You don't need to keep worrying about it."

"It's not that," I say. "Which, I'll still pay you back for it. I just...I think...Steve and I could work things out. Maybe. I'm not sure."

The words seem to slur out of me as I find myself in a surreal alternate universe where I watch helplessly as I break up with someone I love more than life itself. I try to look him straight in the eye, but his eyes seem to divide me, pulling me apart until he can see every part of me that he wants to see. I don't want him to know that all he would have to do is tell me to not get back with Steve. That's all it would take. It's not just a kink that I'll follow his every word—I trust his opinion, especially when it favors something I want. I trust him. And in this case it would mean that I was more to him than a kinky fuck.

He doesn't say anything.

"I mean, Finn, I would be with you in a second, but...everything is so complicated between us. My life has been incredibly complicated and I just need...I need someone who I don't have to share with anyone else or that I don't have to be a hidden mistress to. I'm getting older. I can't just be somebody's fuck buddy and have to hide how much I...how much I like you."

Finn continues to look at me. His shoulders appear slightly tense, but I can't read anything else about his body language.

"It seems like you've made up your mind," he says and then allows several awkward seconds to tick by. "I wish you all the happiness in the world." He leans forward, kissing my forehead, his lips lingering for the shortest second. He takes a step back like he's been hit by lightning. "It's late. We should both go home. I can figure out the foundation issue by myself. I'll see you after the weekend."

I watch him walk back to the elevator, knowing the distance between us now is much farther than a few dozen feet.

******

"You need to tell your boss you're done working for him."

Steve had been insistent that I leave my apartment to move into his, which is ridiculous because my lease wasn't up for another few months, but when I questioned him on it, he reminded me about the recording.

Now, as I sit on his couch that has a stain on it that looks vaguely like Tennessee, I let myself fall into this place where any personal feelings or thoughts vacate my mind. If I let myself think or feel too much, I might die from the tidal wave of it all.

"I still need money for groceries and my phone bill," I say, the calculations floating through my head. "My job pays well enough that I can cover part of the rent too and—"

"No," he cuts in. "I can pay for that. You don't need a cell phone. I can pay for groceries too. Besides, the only reason he paid you well is because you were fucking him. You were just an overpriced prostitute. You didn't even have any experience in administrative work. It was clearly just a cover. If you had any dignity or self-respect, you'd have quit already."

I grit my teeth, but I let it go. I can still hear my voice in the recording, reminding me how stupid I was to talk about my relationship with Finn to Steve. I should have realized something was up when he was asking for details. And maybe he's right. If I was stupid enough to fall for Steve's trap, maybe I didn't realize anything weird about how I kept a job I wasn't qualified for and had no experience in doing.

I can feel Steve wearing me down. He knows what he's doing. I stand, walking to his refrigerator. He says that he can cover the cost of groceries, but he only ever seems to have condiments, beer, and boxes of leftovers

in his fridge. It's the standard of his whole apartment—
he has nothing of substance, but that doesn't mean he
doesn't indulge in short-term pleasures. There's a whole
bookshelf of video games, a large poster of an anime
girl above his couch, and what appeared to be porn
magazines that solely focused on the fetish of women
dressed as babies.

I grab one of the beers. I twist off the cap,
listening to the satisfying hiss as the pressure is released.
At least something around here can decompress.

"Get me a beer too, bitch" Steve calls out.

I take a slow breath and open the refrigerator
again as I hear the TV turn on and the voices of some
reality TV show contestants complain about the
conditions of their house. I close my eyes, pretending
I'm actually with Finn. The demands would all be part
of a game—maybe I'd bring him a beer without twisting
off the cap and he'd pretend to be mad about it. He'd
grab me, yanking me onto the comfort of his lap. His
hand would come down like lightning, striking me hard
enough that it would sound like thunder.

"Sarah!" Steve yells. I twist off the cap of the
beer. I walk back into the living room and hand it to
him. He takes it without looking at me and drinks in a
sip. "You shouldn't even do a two week notice. Just tell
him you're done."

"I'm going to need him later for a
recommendation when I apply for other jobs—"

"I told you I could pay for your expenses. You should be happy. That's more than what that asshole did."

I stare at him. I try to remember how he used to be when we first started dating. After he began changing—his jealousy rising up if I even glanced at another man, constantly talking down to me, his anger flashing up to a point that I was always prepared for him to stroke out—I thought it was my fault. It was my first real relationship and he was older than me, so I assumed he knew better. I kept my gaze down, so there was no risk of looking at other men. I took his scrutiny as constructive criticism and tried to improve myself. When he was angry, I asked for forgiveness, even when I knew he was being oversensitive. He'd always eventually forgive me, but only after he had spent a few hours reminding me of how I had messed up again and how no one else could ever love me. I spent a lifetime wanting a Prince Charming and Steve's neurotic devotion felt like a prince's love at the time.

"He wasn't an asshole," I mutter, unable to stop the words. Steve grips his beer bottle tighter.

"Tell him you're not coming in tomorrow or ever again!"

"At least let me quit my job by telling him to his face."

He grabs his cell phone. I already know what's he's going to do, but I wince anyway when I hear my voice through his recording.

I don't know if I'd definitely call it a relationship, but sure, it could be called that.

"This is for your own good, Sarah. You know how you are. You always run headfirst into danger and I'm just helping you avoid that," Steve says in a raised voice that sounds raspy from overuse. "Call him. Now."

He slides his cell phone back into his pocket. I'd already tried to sneak into his phone to delete the recording, but his phone is locked with a password. He watches me, waiting.

I take my cellphone off his couch armrest. I find Finn's number. My finger hovers over it for a few seconds, my heart beating a lot harder than it should be and my mouth opens for air to leave as I fight off breaking down into sobs.

I press the call button and bring the phone up to my ear. I feel my face getting hot. I wish I could have this conversation in private with Finn, but the way that Steve is staring at me tells me that he expects to hear every word of this conversation.

"Hello," Finn answers. I swallow. He knows it's me or else he would have answered more professionally, but he didn't call me *baby girl* either, which tells me he's already accepted our break-up. He's moved on like I knew he would.

"I, uh, wanted to talk about work."

"Okay."

"I don't think—I don't...I'm not coming in tomorrow."

"Are you sick?" The trace of genuine concern in his voice is enough to wreck me. I was *never* just a fuck to him. I turn away from Steve. I'll deal with the consequences of that later.

"No. I meant that...I'm not coming in anymore."

"You're quitting."

"Yes."

"If it's because you don't think we can work together without having sex, I am certain that we can."

"It's not that. I'm just...quitting."

"I don't understand."

"You don't need to," I say. "I just wanted you to know. I'm sorry. I hope Marge is able to take over my responsibilities."

I hear the couch creak as Steve stands up. I can feel his presence as he approaches and I feel this mix of fear and anger as he steps in front of me. He mimics a gesture of hanging up to me.

"If it's because of Steve—"

"It's not," I say. "I'm so sorry. I have to go."

I hang up. Steve wraps his arm around my waist, pulling me in front of him and his groin rubs up against my ass. Disgusted with myself, I pull away from him.

"It's that time of the month," I say, though I've been skipping the placebo pills from my birth control packs. Still, Steve wrinkles his nose and whispers,

"Yuck, to himself before retreating to the couch. When he first proposed sex, I told him I had a stomachache. He can't read me at all. I know I can't hold him off forever, but I don't know how I could get through it without thinking about Finn and holding on to the idea of Finn without getting to be near him might be worse than having to sleep with Steve.

At least with Steve, I can exist as a numb body. When I think about Finn, my whole heart seems to encompass everything else and every inch of it is straining for Finn, knowing it won't ever reach him.

Chapter 15
RUNNING ON EMPTY

In order for me to say the sex was bad would require Steve to have lasted more than a few minutes. It's essentially the same as it was when we were in a relationship, but that was before I had slept with Finn. When I thought there was supposed to be the pinching pain as he pushed into me dry and I thought men would always, inevitably get off after a few minutes and if I wanted any pleasure, I'd have to do it myself.

For a time, I thought sex was just a way to assuage men's anger or convince them that I was truly apologetic for whatever offense he thought I had committed. I lost the expectation of a man caring about it being pleasurable for me or giving a shit about my desires and fantasies.

I lie next to him, hearing his snoring as he sleeps. I slip out of bed, grabbing my laptop off the bedside table. I sneak out to the living room. As I sit down on the couch, I notice the drawing of the anime girl above me. Now that I've seen it a few times, I notice that she has the same dark, long hair as me, the same body shape, the same eye color—she even appears to be wearing the same waitress uniform I used to wear.

I shrug it off, turning on my laptop and grabbing a beer from the refrigerator. *Nothing matters* has become a mantra in my life and I've gotten used to beer being a main source of hydration. If this is my life now, I might as well be tipsy through the whole thing.

I log in to Tumblr. I had changed my username to *BadBabyGirl22*. I had mentioned my account to Finn once, but I'm still surprised to see *DaddyFinn has started following you.*

I could message him directly, but if Steve ever found out, he'd blow a gasket. Still, if he's following me, maybe he'll read what I post. He'd almost have to see it.

I click on the icon to start a text post. My fingers loom over the keyboard. I check over my shoulder, listening to be certain that Steve is still snoring.

I miss you.

I delete the words. It's too obvious. And maybe Finn just decided to follow me on a whim after creating an account. Yet there's a flicker of hope in me because of his username. Unless he's telling all of the women he fucks to call him Daddy, it would seem to indicate that he only intends to follow me. I click on his username. He hasn't posted or reblogged anything.

I return to the text post.

Love wasn't meant to exist so briefly.

I press *post* before I overthink it and the text appears at the top of my dashboard. There's so much more I wish I could say, and I might have only accomplished confusing him, but since silence is my new ideology, I finish my beer. When I get up to get another one, I find only one remaining—solitary between the mustard and a Chinese takeout box. I don't want to deal with Steve's mood when he finds out there's no beer left, so I grab my bag. There's a 24/7 grocery store that's a couple blocks away that sells Steve's brand of beer and liquor.

******

Apparently, the grocery store stops selling liquor from between 12:01 am to 7:59 am, but beer is always purchasable, so I buy two cases before trudging back to Steve's apartment.

Steve's neighborhood is nice in the way that there's minimal fear of being robbed or killed in a drive-by, but it's also not a white picket fence community, where everyone waves as you walk by and everyone knows you by name. Except for a few men, my old neighbors didn't even look at me. They kept their heads bowed like they'd rather not get involved.

I unlock the door to Steve's apartment with one of the packs of beer under my arm. I quietly close the door behind me and carry the beers to the kitchen. As I put them in the refrigerator, I hear Steve's stomping footsteps. Before I can turn around, he's grabbed my arm, jerking me around to look at him.

"Where the hell were you?" he demands. "It's not even six o'clock."

"You were almost out of beer. I just got two cases—"

"At five in the morning? Bullshit." He spits as he talks, a fleck of saliva landing on my nose. I restrain from wiping it off, knowing the slightest movement could cause him to explode. "You went to see him, didn't you, you nasty slut?"

"Who?" I ask, but I already know. Finn is always in the front of my mind.

"Your boss," he sneers. "You just loved being his little whore, so you went back for more. Or were you so desperate, you'd fuck just any guy willing now?"

"I was just getting the beer—"

He slaps me across the face so quickly that at first, all I feel is sharp heat. My old thoughts creep into my mind: *of course, it's my fault. He should be suspicious of me leaving the house in the middle of the night. He's just insecure and he needs me to reassure him. He's broken and I can fix him. I can get him to love me.*

But the thoughts feel forced and ruined by the sharp edges of our history. This confrontation was bound to occur at some point, he was just waiting for the opportunity. But, he has the recording and his mental instability means that I can't trust his reaction if I don't play the role he expects me to play.

"I'm sorry," I lower my gaze. "I know I've given you no reason to trust me and you have every reason to distrust me. I messed up. I won't leave in the middle of the night again. I'll...we'll go to the store together next time."

He crosses his arms over his chest. "How is that going to help? You'll just say you're going to the bank or the fucking hardware store while you're trying to suck his dick!"

"I—I don't know what you want me to say."

"You can't even be trusted at your job you pathetic bitch. Why the hell would I trust you to go anywhere else?"

"I can't just stay in the apartment, Steve."

"You can leave the apartment. I'll just go with you on days you're allowed," he says. He smiles and I'm reminded of every movie serial killer's smile before he murders his victim. "You know I want what's best for you, Sarah. Once we get this wild child version of you under control, you can trust yourself to not use sex to feed your self-esteem. You just need to get a healthy mindset and until then, you can trust me to guide you. I've known you long enough that I know what's best for you. You know that, right?"

I grip my fists in front of me. "Of course. You're

right."

He moves forward, his lips pressing hard against mine before his tongue jabs against my teeth. He tries to get his tongue in my mouth again. I don't want to invoke his anger, so I let it slip between my teeth, ignoring my instinct to bite down. I try to imagine that he's Finn—that the slap was foreplay and everything that happened was just a way to arouse me—but it just causes an ache inside me, reminding me of how far I've fallen and what I can never get back.

******

"Steve," I hear Erin's irritated voice at the doorway. "I know she's in there. I heard her before I knocked. I just want to talk to her."

"You tried to break us up last time. You're just a bitch who wants her to be miserable and hates our love!"

"If you want to see a bitch, I will show you a bitch, Steve."

I hear Steve stumble backward. Erin must have pushed him out of the way. I pretend to be consumed in the methodology of pouring blueberries into a pie crust. Erin enters the kitchen and sidles up right beside me while I pretend she doesn't exist. It's not that I'm upset or angry that she's here—it's a salvation to see someone I know who isn't Steve—but I don't need her to tell me how bad my situation is or that I shouldn't be staying with Steve just to help Finn or for my own self-preservation. I had told Erin I was going to be moving back in with Steve, but Steve had told me to block her number a week after I moved in with him because she was a 'bad influence on me,' so we hadn't spoken in a while.

"Hey, Sarah," Erin says, her voice coming out like she's talking to a bird with a broken leg. "How are you?"

"I'm doing great," I say, trying to avoid the sarcasm that's dying to break through. Steve lumbers into the kitchen, plucking a blueberry out of the pie crust. I can sense Erin glaring at him.

"You hate blueberry pie," Erin says. "And you hate baking."

"Steve is helping me to find new hobbies. He wants me to concentrate on productive pastimes."

"I'm sure he does." Erin turns toward Steve. "Steve, don't you have a job to go to or something?"

"Why? Did you think that I wouldn't be here when you knocked?" Steve glances between us. "Did you two plan this out?"

"No, definitely not," I mumble, rolling the dough for the crust. "You know I wouldn't do anything like that behind your back."

"Actually, I don't know that. Erin, if you must know, I just came back for lunch. Sarah misses me when I'm gone so I come home to be with her. I do have to get back to work, but I can certainly escort you out of my own apartment."

"Steve…" Erin shakes her head. "I swear to God, someday karma is going to track you down and give you exactly what you deserve."

"Good," he says. "I'll be waiting for that sweet, sweet raise and a woman whose first instinct isn't to fuck her boss. Thank you, Erin, for that good news. Let's go."

He puts his hand on her shoulder, trying to push her toward the door, but Erin shrugs his hand off.

"Sarah, if you ever need anything, just call me," she says. She bites her lower lip. "I miss you."

Erin spins around, walking back to the entrance door. I hear it open, then slam shut. The whole apartment seems to rattle.

"That woman is poison," Steve says. "She doesn't want you to get better. She likes having somebody to look down on."

There's a part of me that knows he's trying to manipulate me, but another part that tugs at my brain. Erin has always been in healthy relationships and lived a happy life. Why would she be friends with a mess like me? She has no benefit from it. Maybe this is the one thing that Steve is right about. Maybe every single person in my life just looks at me and thinks about how they can save me.

If I wasn't crazy before, I'm slowly losing my

mind now. I just wish I could see Finn one more time before I'm put in a straitjacket and all that's left of me is this empty shell.

******

At night, I dream of Finn. I dream of his mouth, his hands, his voice, his scent, his presence—all of it. I fall asleep, trying to figure out how to control my dreams, so I can tell him everything I want to tell him and make him happy one more time. I want to commit acts with him that he'd never, ever forget—Bonnie and Clyde sinful acts that would leave him gasping for air.

I roll over in bed, after a particularly good dream about Finn. I press my fingertips against my ass, trying to recall the feeling of his discipline, trying to remember how well-administered pain could be the perfect paradox of pleasure, and how when you trust someone, even pain can be appreciated.

A couple of minutes pass before I remember that Steve never made it back home last night. It was a little disappointing because I had wanted to get out of the apartment for the night—maybe go to a restaurant or just to the gas station—but he never returned and never texted me to tell me where he was.

It's been about a month and a half since I moved in, so I'm not naive to what he's doing when he's gone until the early hours. I've seen the texts from random women with heart emojis, smelled the perfume, heard the lazy lies, and seen the pair of earrings in his car's cup holder. I wish I could say that I didn't care. I mostly don't, but there's viciousness to knowing I'm not enough to keep the one man happy who actually wants me or whatever it is that he feels for me. I wasn't enough for Finn and I'm not enough for Steve. I'm just someone to fuck or else Finn would've reached out to me on Tumblr after my post that was clearly for him.

So, I drink and sleep. I cry, which I could blame on the alcohol, but I'd have nobody to justify it too. I've reposted quotes on Tumblr, other people's words encompassing my emotions better than I can, but I can't even tell if Finn has logged in recently. I wrote the last post, talking about Dante's *Inferno* and how everyone in Hell deserved to be there, so it makes sense that I'm in the ninth circle. I don't have any hope that Finn will see it anymore—I just need to feel like my words have some permeance and I'm not a ghost that only Steve sees.

My cell phone, placed on the edge of my nightstand, illuminates the whole room as a notification comes in. I grab it, the screen so bright it's hard to read, but the first word I register is *Finn*. A new text. It's the first one I've gotten from him since I told him I was quitting.

I unlock my screen to read the whole message.
How are you?
I try to read between those words. Is it simply a

formality? No, I don't think he would text an ex-employee or a fuck buddy just to ask how they're doing—unless he has ulterior motives. Maybe he just wants another hook-up. Maybe I didn't send him all of the information he needed for his next assistant. Maybe he's just lonely and all his other women are busy flying first-class or eating hors d'oeuvres with politicians.

I type *I'm good. How are you?* but I don't hit send. It feels wrong to lie to him, but if I tell him things aren't great—well, he'd be smart to take off running in the opposite direction. He'd think I was a drama queen, desperate to get pity for my own mistakes and he doesn't deserve to be brought down by me.

I hit send.

I stare at his text. *How are you?* What would I say to him if I was being honest? *I miss you. You could make this better. Do you remember that time you took care of me at the hospital? That feeling of worthiness is starting to fade and I'm afraid I'll forget what it feels like.*

I love you.

I love you.

God, I love you.

When the little dots appear, telling me he's typing back, I sit up. I ignore the feeling of the cold around me and the longing that he was beside me now.

I'm alright. Did you find a new job? I expected to give my praises to other employers, but I never received any calls.

I hesitate. I don't want him to know I'm not working. It could only be interpreted badly—that I'm either lazy, dependent on someone, or only with someone so that he can pay for my necessities.

I text back, *I'm glad you're happy.*

I hear the front door open. My heart feels crushed in my chest as I delete the messages. Steve checks my phone too often for me to risk him finding it. I turn off my phone. If he looks at it, I can pretend that it died.

Steve stumbles in, his shirt buttoned wrong and his fly open. I've wondered if he purposefully doesn't hide his infidelity, just to remind me of my powerlessness and inferiority. In the past—when we had a legitimate relationship—it worked on me too well. I'd cry and yell at him, I'd swear I'd never forgive him if he did it again, he'd apologize, and then he'd do it again, just to prove he knew my threats were empty.

I thought love was supposed to be this way: a constant power struggle where I'd always have to feel like everything I said, did, and felt was invalid. It was only with Finn that had a lover who had all the power in the world and never abused a single inch of it. His power empowered me. And I have to find a way to forget that.

"Hey, Sarahhhh," Steve drawls. He clambers onto the bed next to me, the mix of body odor and beer enough to make me wonder who on earth would want to have sex with him. "How'd I know you'd be up waiting for me to give you what you need?"

"I don't need anything."

"Yes, you do," he says, the finality in his voice enough to remind me of every other time I've confronted him and it failed to make any difference. I don't move the rest of the night. Steve rocks over me like a broken rocking horse and the only way I can cope is thinking about what Finn would text back to me. Maybe I should have added a question to keep the conversation going. Maybe I shouldn't have answered at all. I'm just a drug addict, buying the drug over and over, knowing I'll never be able to inject it but wallowing in the anticipation.

I don't fall asleep. Around 5 a.m., I grab my phone and turn it back on. There's one new text from Finn.

Do you want to meet for coffee?

Chapter 16
HIDEAWAY

Steve made me install an app on my phone that's called BabysitterEyes 2.0. It's meant to keep track of my movements since he doesn't trust me not to sneak around with random men while he's at work. I could leave the phone at the apartment, but he also calls nearly every half hour and rampages if I don't pick up before it goes to voice mail. Fortunately, since I have the app on my phone, I can also track my own movements and I know that the app isn't good enough to recognize when I'm in the coffee shop across the street.

I've only risked it once before since Steve wouldn't let me leave the apartment for nearly a week, but now I have more incentive. Now, I have a chance to embed every little thing about Finn into my memory. Maybe he would even touch me and I can remember what it feels like to be so enthralled.

I get to the coffee shop five minutes earlier than the time Finn and I had agreed to. I run my fingers through my hair, trying to use my phone's camera to make sure I look good. I don't. The drinking, sleeping, and only being able to pace in the apartment has turned me into this zombie-version of myself. My skin is a little grayish, my hair isn't as smooth, and my bones are a bit more prominent under my skin.

This was a mistake.

I don't want Finn to remember me like this. I don't want him to look at me and wonder what the hell he ever saw in me. I don't want him to think that I'm falling apart, which he will know because he can always look at me and know exactly what's going on in my head. It's mostly what made him so damn good in bed.

The bell above the coffee shop door jingles. I see Finn step in. He looks even better than I remember. He reminds me of those depictions of the Greek gods, all muscle with the defined jaws and the dirty blonde hair that's effortless, but every strand emphasizes the perfect structure of his face.

God, I've forgotten what arousal feels like. As he turns toward me, I bow my head, so my hair falls in front of my face. If I can't cancel this meeting, the least I could do is try to look more presentable by hiding myself. Even as I feel his body heat stop in front of the table, I don't look up.

"Sarah."

His voice comes out like a command and I can't help but do as he says. His eyes take me by surprise like they always do and I nearly break into tears. I can feel the chill of the ocean water and the heat of a beach just looking at them. I can imagine myself in a bikini with his body on top of me, kissing me until I forget the last month and a half.

He reaches forward, his hand resting on my arm for a moment before he sits down across from me.

"Did you get something to drink?" he asks. I shake my head.

"I don't...I don't have any extra money right now."

"I'll pay for it."

"You don't need to."

"I want to," he says. He leans back against the booth. "You seemed sad when we were texting."

I tilt my head, astonished that he could possibly gather that from my vague texts. Then I remember that I'm trying to hide my zombie face. I duck my head back down. "What makes you think I was sad?"

"I know you, Sarah. When we used to text, you didn't censor your thoughts at all. I'd get five different texts on my phone and none of them were relevant to each other."

"I'm sorry about that."

"I liked that about you," he says, his voice softening. "I live in a world where everyone triple checks what they say. I never thought you'd be sending me a text that said *I'm good. How are you?*"

"I'm sorry—" I stop myself. "Maybe I just didn't

feel talkative last night."

"Are you saying that you're happy?"

I don't look at him. The waitress steps up to the table and Finn orders two coffees. After she leaves, I realize his phone hasn't made any noise since he's been here. He must have turned it off or put it on silent, which feels incredibly kind to me. He always has a million people he needs to be in constant contact with and the fact that he'd turn off his phone for me seems like a bigger step of dedication than an average man would show by proposing.

"I didn't just ask to meet you because I was concerned—which, I am. Your friend, Erin, got ahold of me and she was deeply concerned about your relationship with…Steve."

The disdain in his voice when he says Steve's name gives me a tiny flutter of pleasure. But maybe I should be more loyal to Steve—he has paid for the roof over my head and food—but I've felt more loyal to Finn than anyone else since the day we met. It's at least half the reason I'm with Steve to begin with.

"If he's doing anything bad to you, you know I can help you out. If you need a place to stay or someone to talk to, we can figure it out."

"I'm okay," I say.

"Erin said that you haven't even been talking to her."

"I've been busy."

"She said Steve was abusive before."

"He's changed."

The defenses come to me naturally—months and months of trying to justify my own actions. If I let him know the real reason, he'll do something stupid and I can't allow that. This is the one thing I can do for him that will pay him back for all the ways he has changed my life.

He reaches across the table, taking my hand. My hand feels incomparably cold compared to his. He takes a deep breath.

"You are much more to me than I've let you know," he says. "I should have told you sooner. I'm sorry."

My heart feels like it could drive right through my rib cage and spatter all over his chest. This is all I've wanted to hear, but it hurts. It's one thing to think that all I've ever wanted is something I can't have and that he would never give it to me anyway, but it's another to know I can't have it, but that he actually would give me everything I want and more.

Finn takes off his luxury watch. He sets it on the table between us. I flush as I see the scratches in the glass. I still haven't paid him back for it and Steve definitely won't pay that expense for me.

"I've had a couple of friends ask me about the scratches on this," Finn says. "They ask me why I haven't replaced the glass on such a nice watch. I don't give them any actual answer. Do you remember making those scratches?"

"Of course," I blurt. "And I'll find a way to pay you back for it, I swear—"

"Sarah," Finn interjects. "The watch is more valuable to me with the scratches. I think of you every time I look at it."

Again, only a herculean effort prevents me from releasing into sobs. Tears well up in my eyes, but I blink them away. Everything I want is so, so close to me and yet he has never been so far away. It makes me feel like there are a thousand doves inside my heart, but they're stuck and unable to get out, causing a chaotic pain inside me.

He takes my hand. "I love you."

"I love you too," I say before I can stop myself. I close my eyes, trying not to cry. I feel him squeeze my hand.

"I know this is terrible timing. I know you're with another guy, but I had to tell you the truth."

All I can do is nod as our coffee arrives at our table. He thanks the server and slowly releases my hand. He sits back and lifts his mug, taking the smallest sip to test the heat. I add sugar and cream to mine, focusing on simply breathing in and out to prevent me from having God-knows-what kind of break down.

I brush away any trace of tears and sit up straight. "I have to tell you something, but you have to promise me that you won't react badly."

"If this has anything to do with how Steve is treating you, I promise nothing."

"It doesn't," I say. "I mean…"

The muscles in his arms tense like a super hero preparing to morph into an invisible god-like creature in order to save the world. I take a deep breath.

"It's more about you," I say. "Steve knows about…that we were sleeping together."

"Okay."

I take a sip of my coffee, trying to figure out how to tell him the truth. I'll just have to blunder through it.

"Steve says he knows a board member of *Torv Global* who hates you and wants to replace you with his son. He—Steve—came over about a month and a half ago and…I hadn't realized he was recording our conversation, but he has a recording, which has me saying that we had a relationship together. And Steve is certain that this board member could convince the other board members that the company should fire you and sue you for sexual harassment or misconduct or something. Steve is convinced that even if I refused to go along with this allegation of sexual harassment, the board would still fire and sue you on behalf of the company. You would be fired in disgrace and might go to jail in addition to paying fines. You'd never be hired as a CEO again. And I'd become a pariah. Nobody would hire a woman that causes sexual harassment suits to be filed or anyone who could be seen as trying to sleep their way to the top."

Finn's jaw is rigid. He sets his coffee mug down. "And he's using all of that to trap you into staying with him."

I nod. "It's just a mess. I'm so, so sorry, Finn."

"Do you think there's a way to delete that recording?"

"He's very protective of his phone. It's password protected and I wouldn't be surprised if he had uploaded the recording to a website or something."

"So, you couldn't just destroy the phone."

"I don't think it would help," I say, my voice coming out as small as I feel. "He would've thought of that. I'm sorry."

"You don't need to apologize," he says. "None of this is your fault."

"If I had been smart enough to know he had been recording me—"

"It's his fault," Finn cuts me off. "He couldn't make you fall in love with him, so he decided to blackmail and basically kidnap you so that he could..."

Finn goes silent. His jaw is tense and his eyes burn with what I would describe as anger in any other person, but what seems much deeper and more like righteous indignation coming from him.

"There has to be some dirt on him," he continues. "If we can counter-blackmail him, it could solve our problem."

"I…I don't know what you could find on him," I say. I can feel myself wilting like an unwatered dandelion.

"It's the only choice we have. Unfortunately, he is right. Though it's not fair, if this gets out, it would ruin us both professionally. Why don't you come to my house? We can figure out everything from there."

"I can't," I say. "He keeps track of my phone—"

His right hand coils into a fist. "Are you kidding me?"

I shake my head. "The only reason I could come here is because the apps shows that I'm still at the apartment. He lives in that building across the street. I should actually be getting back there now. He usually comes home for lunch around 11:30."

I stand, shifting my gaze away from him. When I came here, I wanted to memorialize him. Now, after speaking aloud about the damage I could do to his life, I think it's best to forget him. And for him to forget me.

"I think it's best that we go our separate ways now," I say, my voice cracking.

I turn to walk away, but he grabs my wrist. Electricity surges under my skin and I can't help but think that I could have felt this way every day of my life if I hadn't told Steve about Finn and me.

"I'll fix this," he promises and it's the first time I've *ever* doubted his words.

******

When I was eleven, I lost my father to a motorcycle accident. At first, my mother stayed in bed, but after a week or so, she acted like nothing had happened. She told me that depression was just a word and anything could be overcome with the right attitude. I believed her until I was so deep in denial that my numbness could only be overcome by high levels of adrenaline, drugs, or pain.

And now I can feel myself struggling to exist between this place of numbness and of depression. When I'm numb, all I can think about is how Finn ignited something inside of me that destroyed the fogginess in my head and that my body aches for it. When I'm depressed, my heart aches.

I flip my pillow for the third time tonight. Steve is gone again. I've started to worry about STDs, but there's no way I could bring up condoms to him without him blowing up.

I close my eyes. I remember the feeling of Finn's hand around my wrist. I slip my fingers under the elastic of my panties. I rub around my clit, sliding my fingers inside me. I try to pretend they're Finn's fingers. I try to imagine him fucking me like he knows it's the last time. I imagine him resting his cock against my lips and I'd pretend to resist until he put his hands around my throat, giving increasing pressure until I opened my lips. I open my legs wider, rubbing harder, but I know it's pointless. With Steve's pitiful attempts at thrusting a few times before coming, I've tried a dozen times to pleasure myself. I can reach arousal, but nothing past that. It's like crawling through a desert until I've reached an oasis, only to realize that it is a mirage.

The front door slams shut. I slide my hand back under my pillow and pretend to be asleep. I hear the bedroom light switch on and Steve's footsteps come closer to me. After several seconds pass without any more noise or feeling him touch me, I open my eyes enough to see slit versions of Steve. He's checking my phone.

He sets the phone back down and I close my eyes again. He grabs my shoulder, shaking it. I pretend to slowly wake-up. He doesn't wait, pulling off his pants and boxers before straddling me. Something in me— something past the numbness and the depression—rips through me.

"Get off me," I snap, shoving him. He stumbles off me, fumbling to grab some blankets to cover his groin as if he thinks I'm going to kick it.

"What's your problem?"

I get out of the bed, grabbing the sweater I had been wearing earlier. I jerk it over my head, pulling it on. "I don't want to sleep with you right now. That's it."

He gets off the bed too, his face getting red.

"Yeah, well, what about what I want, you selfish bitch?"

"All I do is give you what you want! You've taken everything!"

"You never give me what I want! You lie there like a fish when we fuck and you never say anything nice to me! I bet when you were fucking your boss, you did acrobatics for him. I bet you constantly praised him like he was a god. What was so great about him, huh? It's because of his money, right, you gold digging whore?"

"No, it's not."

"Yeah, that's what it is, it's all that damn money," he sneers as if I had said nothing at all. He begins to pace around the room, his movements tense and mechanical. "And those pretty boy looks. If he didn't look like he just stepped out of some fancy pretty boy magazine you wouldn't care."

"Bullshit," I say, letting my anger get the best of me. The back of my neck tingles as I feel an insistent desire to defend Finn from Steve's attacks. I expect him to lash out, but he just rolls his eyes.

"You like the status, the fancy restaurants, the trips, this other world that your Sugar Daddy gave you. You're so damn high-maintenance. You want to be a princess when you act like a streetwalker!"

"No, you're just fucking wrong!"

"Then why? Why the hell do you want him so much?!"

"It's because of who he is inside! You hear me?! It's because of who he fucking is!" I yell into his face.

His hand comes at me like a slingshot. I crumple onto the floor, clinging to the heat on my cheek as my ears ring. He crouches beside me and grabs my wrist, forcing my hand away from my cheek.

"If you ever talk to me that way again, I will show you how I treat streetwalkers. You're no longer in a castle, you dirty bitch, so you better learn how to act."

He lets go of my wrist. I listen to him turn off the light and crawl into bed. I stay on the floor, listening to my heartbeat.

Did he just admit to using prostitutes?

Chapter 17
GLIMMER

As a salesman, Steve survives on how people perceive him. He knows how to fake empathy and feign interest.

When we first began dating, I used to think that's why he would come home angry and disinterested in my life—he'd used up all of his charm and love on customers. It's not until I realized his temper stayed calm when he was out with his friends or when we visited his parents that I began to doubt my reasoning.

Even then, I knew it was pointless to explain this volatile side of him because people knew him as a funny, endearing man. Steve was still paranoid that I would spread 'slander' against him, so he slowly convinced me that everyone would think I was an over-dramatic woman who craved attention if I ever said anything bad about him.

Perception is everything to him, but if I had the ability to destroy his good-ole-American-boy reputation, it could get him to delete his recording of me confirming my relationship with Finn.

Steve steps out of the shower, his towel wrapped around his waist. I can feel him seething as he watches me pull the sheets off the bed. Ever since that night he confronted me about my feelings for Finn, he's had the shortest fuse I've ever seen him have. I've always been able to predict his rages with some range of certainty, but now it seems like he's always ready to erupt.

"My boss cut back my hours," he says. "So, you're going to need to get off your lazy ass and get a job."

I nod, not daring to say anything even in agreement. He's found ways to twist my words against me, finding ways to constantly victimize himself with the impassive words I say. I've found silence can be a tourniquet—enough to stop the bleeding, but not enough to completely save me from any situation.

He doesn't say anything else. I hear his drawers open as he gets dressed. I move the sheets to the hamper. I hand him his wallet and phone as he approaches the door, his hair still wet. He gives me a stiff kiss on the cheek before opening the door. I mumble a goodbye before walking over to the north window. I peer out, watching him get into his car. After he drives away, I slip on my shoes.

I shiver as I step outside. It's a bit colder than I had expected. I wait for a car to pass by before crossing the road. I walk into the coffee shop across from Steve's apartment, striding straight up to the cashier. I ask to use the shop's phone. The cashier allows it and I dial Erin's number.

"Hello?" she answers.

"Hey, it's Sarah."

"Oh, God, Sarah, how are you? Do you need help? Can I come get you?"

"I do need help," I say. "I need help catching Steve with a…with a hooker."

"I'm sorry?"

"It's a long story," I say. "But I'm hoping you can track Steve after he leaves work. I'll pay you back for it somehow, but I need to figure out where he goes at night. For the last several nights, he hasn't returned home and he smells like perfume. I…I just have my doubts that he's been able to pick up a woman every night."

Erin snorts. "I'm surprised he's able to pick up any women ever."

"Whoever he does pick up, it's because they don't know him. So can you do it?"

"I think so," she says. "Do you want me to just keep following him until I find a prostitute or…?"

I hear a muffled voice in the background.

"It's Sarah," I hear Erin say. "Sorry, Sarah, it's Tom. I'm sure he can help too."

"Just be careful," I say. "Steve has been really angry lately. I'd hate for either of you to get into any kind of trouble."

"You know I have no problem doing this for you."

"Thank you."

"Of course, Sarah. Are you doing okay?"

"Yeah," I lie. "But I have to go. We'll talk soon, okay? I'll call you back in a few days. If you have anything urgent to tell me, you can text me early in the morning or later in the afternoon—I'd just be careful though. His work schedule has been erratic and he seems more suspicious of me than he's been before."

"You're the one who needs to be careful, Sarah."

"I know," I say. "Thanks for your help, Erin."

"Absolutely."

"We'll talk later."

"I'll be here."

I hang up. I feel like I'm standing on two geological faults and I know the earthquake is coming.

The road is busier when I leave the coffee shop. I have to wait a couple minutes before I can cross the road. It just makes me more nervous—being a spy and working behind people's backs isn't something I have ever wanted to do. But, in the end, I know it comes down to Steve or Finn and me. Thinking that Steve will permanently keep from using the recording to hurt Finn is naïve at best. Even if I continue to stay willingly in this sick mixture of being held hostage and being enslaved, he can't help himself. He will use the recording to hurt Finn and expect me to carry on if nothing had happened. Steve's word is worthless. I can't let Finn suffer for my mistakes, but I also don't think I can survive without him much longer since I've learned that he loves me too.

When I get back to Steve's apartment, my phone vibrates. I look down at the screen.

It's a text from Finn.

Erin called me.

Erin has become talkative since I've begun living with Steve. Another notification pops up onto my screen.

Have things gotten worse? Do you need me to come get you?

As wary as I am to have him contacting me, there's a reassurance in knowing he's thinking of me. It almost feels like it used to be.

I text back. *I'm okay. I may have just found a way out of this.*

How? I can help.

He may be involved with prostitutes.

You think that's enough to get him to back off?

I hesitate. His doubt becomes mine. *I hope so.*

I can have some people look into it.

That might help, but aren't you worried your people will become suspicious about why you're looking into him?

No.

I lie down on the couch. I try to think of what to

text him—what to tell him that would keep him in love with me. I feel my phone vibrate in my hand.

I miss you.

I swallow. *I miss you too.* That's the biggest understatement of my entire life.

Several minutes pass. I scroll through our messages, rereading his words like a high-schooler unfolding a love letter to read it for the third time. He's so good to me that I can almost believe I deserve it. An exclamation mark appears, telling me there's a new message. I scroll back down.

I've dreamt of you the last couple of nights.

I smile. *Oh? Was I a saint or a sinner?*

I wait impatiently for him to reply. He has to be working right now, so I shouldn't be consumed in what he has to say, but it feels so good to pretend we haven't changed from a couple months ago and it feels even better to be wanted by someone like him. He dreams of me at night, but I've dreamt of him and him wanting me back since the day we met.

Dots appear as he types. I close my eyes, imagining his body drenched over mine and his breath on my neck.

Definitely a sinner, though you were dressed in white last time. The first dream, you didn't text me to tell me you were home safe, so when you came into work, I had bought a paddle just for the occasion. You climbed on top of me after and we fucked in the same rhythm as the spanking. You took it very well.

I close my eyes. *I can imagine it too well. I bet every time I slid down your cock, you'd spank me just to feel me tighten around you.*

I place my phone behind me on the arm of the couch and slide my hand under the elastic of my yoga pants. I just wish he was here. He makes me so needy and desperate that it seems natural to explode in ecstasy every time I'm with him.

My phone vibrates. I raise it in front of my face with my other hand and check it. *I'm in a meeting with some advertising executives. You're being very distracting.*

I frown. Really? He's going to get me all hot and bothered, then tell me he's busy?

Another message pops up. *It's just another long list of indiscretions I'll have to punish you for later. Your bottom will be so red it will put McIntosh to shame.*

I move my fingers inside me. *You'd need to break me in after all this time.*

It only takes him a few seconds to type back two words. *Red bottom.*

The imagery is so simple, but I can feel the temperature of my skin rising. I try to imagine his cock, thrusting into me, his hands pinning down my wrists, and his lips stealing every moan from my mouth.

I start to text back when I hear the sound of the

key in our front door's lock. I pull my hand out of my pants and shove my phone in between the couch cushions. I stand, fixing my hair as Steve steps into the apartment.

Paranoia grips me. Maybe he has cameras hidden in the apartment and now he can gloat that I'm just as much of a slut as he said I was. There's no other reason for him to be home already.

"I forgot my wallet," he says, walking past me without a second glance. "Have you seen it? It's usually right on the counter..."

"Maybe it's in your coat pocket," I say, trying to make my voice sound as normal as possible.

"Why the hell would it be there?" he says, checking the pockets of his coat anyway. He glances over at me as I hover in front of the couch. "What are you doing?"

When I don't say anything, he takes a few steps closer. His arms are tensed, reminding me of how much stronger he is than me.

"Did you take my wallet?" he demands. "Did you steal my money?"

"What? Of course not. I don't know where it is. Maybe you left it in your car."

He grabs me by the arm, jerking me so violently that I fall onto the couch and hear my neck pop. He grabs me by the jaw.

"Don't you think I would have seen it if it was in

my car?" he hisses. "Damn, you are so stupid." He pushes my forehead, causing the back of my head to hit against the arm of the chair and I instantly have a headache.

He looks down. I swallow, knowing the only thing he could possibly be feeling is my phone. They say your life flashes before your eyes when you die, but my flashes must be coming early because all I can see is Finn's face, different times I've seen him excited, concerned, and happy.

He reaches under the couch cushion. I watch him pull out my phone, clinging to it with two fingers like it could explode.

"Why is this here?"

I open my mouth, but no words will come out. He unlocks the screen. I want to run, but my feet feel like they've been impaled to the floor.

My stomach feels like it's cramping as I see his finger flick over the screen and the unmistakable pale blue bubbles that indicate texts. As he reads, my breathing feels shallow, but I can't remember how to breathe normally.

As his face starts to get red, I lurch forward, reaching for the phone. He yanks it out of my grasp. After I lunge for it again, he tosses it onto the couch and it bounces onto the floor. As I reach down for it, he grabs me around the waist, slamming my back against the front edge of the couch. As the pain courses through me, Steve grabs onto the waistband of my pants, jerking them down a few inches. I grab onto my panties to keep them on, but it just allows him to yank down my pants to my ankles.

I struggle to get on my feet, but he grabs me by the hair, jerking me backward. I stumble against him and we both fall on the couch. I try to scramble away, but he twists my hair around his hand—pinpricks of pain burning in my scalp—forcing my head down near his thigh.

"That's how you like it, huh?" he demands. He tries to yank down my panties again, but I keep a tight grip on them.

"Stop," I plead, my panic and fear turning into tears. "Please, Steve, please, don't—"

His hand comes down on my ass. It's not as hard as Finn, but there isn't the slightest hint of good intentions or pleasure. He wants to leave me small enough for him to crush into dust. He wants me to be broken.

"Stop!"

He hits me again, a little harder.

"You're so gross," he snarls. "Throwing yourself at men. Begging to let them use you. The fact that you get off on this proves that you're sick. You deserve everything bad that has ever happened to you."

His hand comes down again. It's nothing compared to what Finn can do, but I feel shame wash over me like a tidal wave. I was stupid to think that I could catch Steve doing something bad enough to get him to stop blackmailing me and I was stupid to think that my life could end with a happily ever after. Something is wrong inside me and being with Finn was just a momentary fantasy.

Steve tries to yank down my panties again. I keep my grip on it, but I can hear the fabric beginning to tear.

"Stop!" I yell. I keep yelling it like my opinion would matter to him. As I'm seconds away from holding too useless pieces of fabric, I hear a bang and the sound of splintered wood. Before I can turn to look at the front door, I fall off Steve's lap as he stands up. For a brief moment, I wonder if I've blacked out in panic and my mind concocted Finn breaking into Steve's apartment and the next moment, I see a flicker of pure rage on Finn's face before he slams his fist into Steve's jaw.

The sound of grunts and the rapid sound of flesh hitting flesh fill the apartment. Within seconds, I feel warm blood flick onto my cheek. I stumble back, half-crawling away from the two men fighting.

"Finn," I say, pulling my pants back up. Part of me is grateful that Steve is getting what he deserves, but another part knows that his payback costs more than Finn or I can afford. "Finn!"

Finn has a second of hesitation and my stomach lurches as I see Steve grab one of my hardcover books off the coffee table, slamming it against the side of

Finn's head. Finn jerks backward, giving Steve enough space to stagger onto his feet. Steve nearly knocks me over as he stumbles past me. The door is still open from when Finn broke in and Steve runs out it, leaving a small trail of blood behind him.

"Are you okay?" I crawl over to Finn. He touches his temple, checking for blood, but nods. My body is shaking and I can't be certain if it's from how Steve was treating me or the fight. Finn stands up, going over to the door to close and lock it. I feel the warmth of tears before they start to spill over as if all they were waiting for was for Steve to leave. Finn moves back to me, settling beside me on the carpet. His arm wraps around me. I press my face against his chest, letting the tears stream down. I sob.

"Shhh....he's gone now. Daddy's here, baby girl. Daddy's here."

He holds me until my crying calms, but my breathing remains ragged. I look up at him and, as he gazes down at me, I feel a new wave of guilt. I glance down at my trembling hands.

"Did he hurt you?" Finn asks.

"It was special," I say, my words coming out shaky through my tears.

"What, baby girl? What was special?"

"The spanking," I mumble. "It was ours. It was supposed to only be your hand."

He smirks. "Aw, baby girl, it's not the act that

made it special. It was what we had. It's the way we trusted each other—the intimacy—that made it special. He could never take that away. It will always be special for us."

I nod, curling into a smaller ball as I press myself against him.

"Besides," he teases. "You still had your panties on and I doubt he could pull off leaving the artwork I create on your ass."

I smile, looking back up at him. There's a faint red spot on his forehead from where Steve had hit him, but Steve's face definitely ended up worse. I lean forward and Finn kisses me. Everything washes away as our lips meet and, for the first time, I know for absolute certain that he will always protect me. I close my eyes and let myself savor the moment.

******

When Finn opens the doors to his penthouse, I nearly choke.

"How much does Torv pay you?" I manage to get out as I step onto the marble floor. The immediate aspect I notice is that one side of the apartment is windows, which face out toward part of Central Park and part of the cityscape. The marble under my feet slowly fades into new colors as I enter the living room, which has a beautiful crimson and white rug and a white sectional sofa. There's a fireplace in front of the couch with an intricate mantelpiece but I can see mechanisms that allow a flat-screen TV to be lowered as well. I turn to the kitchen and see the granite countertops, the stainless steel stove, and a four-door refrigerator with a screen built into it, which seems to show a calendar, the weather, and an image of what's inside it.

"They pay me what I'm worth," he says.

"Finn, I know what you're worth and it's a lot more, but this is…" My lips form the word *wow* and he smiles at me.

"I'm glad I showed you the penthouse first instead of the house. If you like this, you might not like the more rustic approach of my house," he says. I shake my head.

"I'll love any place that has you in it." I move toward him, wrapping my arms around his waist. He kisses my temple.

"Does that mean if I'm inside you that you'll become self-absorbed and vain?" he teases. I feel my cheeks warm up.

"Mmm. I don't know. You might have to test it." My whole body is getting hot and my interest in the penthouse is fading now that I can feel his heart beating. I slip my hands under his shirt, feeling his abs. He kisses right below my ear, along my jawline.

"Do you want to see the bedroom?" he asks. I can't nod any faster. He puts his hand on the small of my back, leading me toward the kitchen until we take a turn to the left and I notice a wooden French door I had been too overwhelmed to see before. Finn opens the door and I'm overcome with a feeling of tininess. The bed is massive. There are large closet doors to the left and a white door right beside it, which I assume leads to the bathroom.

"I would have thought your bedroom would be filled with trophies," I say, tucking a strand of hair behind my ear. I had been feeling frisky before, but standing in his bedroom now reminds me that he's likely fucked many women far more experienced and beautiful than me.

"No, my bedroom is for sleeping and entertaining special guests," he says. "And now, it's for you."

His hand curls around my waist and I forget all my insecurities. His mouth moves near my ear, but he doesn't kiss it again.

"I believe I owe you a red bottom."

"I believe you do," I say, a little breathless.

"I'm going to wear your little butt out."

"You'll have to catch me first." I wink before running out of the bedroom. He catches me easily as I turn to run around the sectional sofa. His arm wraps around my waist, pulling me downward, but we drop onto the rug and his body cushions my fall. Without any pause, he plucks me back up, dropping me bottom-first onto the armrest of the sofa like I'm a bundle of clothes.

He grabs onto the waistband of my yoga pants and drags them down. I half expect to feel a flashback of Steve's attack, but I don't feel anything except arousal and joy.

"Look at these panties," he says. I look over my shoulder, remembering that I put on a pair he had bought me—they're pink with a cartoon princess on the front. He grasps them in his hands and rips them off me. I squirm against the couch, pretending to try to get away. He grabs onto my ankles and jerks me back to where I was. He leans over me and I can feel his erection against my ass. He whispers, "Do you feel like a princess?"

"A really bratty one," I manage to say. He laughs. I love that laugh.

"True. We need to knock you down a peg or two."

His first slap is quick and nearly painless, but it's enough to send a jolt through me. The next one is harder and I can imagine the sight of my jiggling ass is enough to send a different kind of lightning strike through him. As hard as it's been without him, I'm glad he now has a clean slate to leave his mark on me and my body isn't as familiar to his spankings as it used to be, so there's a new thrill every time that pain jolts me.

I can't imagine he's been spanking anybody else during our hiatus because his hand comes down like he's a madman and I love it. After every minute or so, he has to grab my ankles and drag me back toward him because my body keeps sliding forward.

His hand thrashes back and forth, slamming against my right ass cheek and lifting up before slamming down on my left. He alters the amount of force and the timing in between each smack, so it jars my body every time. His hand is a paintbrush, a military commander, and pure joy all wrapped into one calloused palm.

The final time he yanks me back, he pulls me so far that my stomach ends up on the armrest. There's a drumbeat between my legs and all I want is to have his cock rammed inside me. He spins me around, so we're face-to-face. I reach for him, but he playfully slaps my hands away. I watch him undo his pants and enjoy the clatter of his belt as it falls to the floor. He kicks off his shoes and his pants while I try to be patient. He indicates to his boxer briefs, where his erection is straining against the material. With reckless eagerness, I pull the briefs down. There's no hesitation as I take his head into my mouth, enjoying the faint saltiness of it. After a few seconds, I move my mouth to his balls, his cock rubbing against my cheek as I'm determined to prove myself to be better than he remembers.

His fingers move to my hair, slipping under it. His hands wrap around my neck. There's a slight pressure against my throat but he only guides my face back to his cock. I envelop the side of his cock with my mouth, moving back and forth over it like I'm playing a harmonica. He groans, his fingers tightening around my hair. As I move back to the head, he pushes me back against the couch.

"Get on all fours," he says. "After all that work I did, I want to see your ass for this."

I drop so fast to my hands and knees that I can feel a twinge of pain in my right knee. Finn doesn't wait long either. I feel his hands on either side of my ass, his grip so tight I can feel his thumbs pressing against new bruises, and his cock pressed against my entrance. When he thrusts in, my back arches and I let out a small *oh* as my pussy contracts around him, gripping around his cock like I've never felt it before.

He thrusts into me so quickly and with such power, I can only imagine him as a starving man that only has an appetite for me. Every time I feel like I'm about to come, he slows his pace, barely moving inside of me. I'm just an instrument he's playing and he knows exactly what strings to pluck to avoid the explosive outro. It's a slow torture, but I'd endure so much worse for this man.

After another moment of being so close to orgasm and his slower pace, he kisses the spot between my shoulder blades. The intimacy of it all is enough to cause my knees to slip out from under me. He wraps his arm underneath me to keep my hips raised. As he returns to a frantic pace, my fingernails dig into the rug. I don't think I can last much longer and he must know that too because he doesn't slow down even as my body tenses and I can feel myself about to fall into perfect scorching bliss.

It hits me harder than any smack could. I let out a noise that could only be compared to crooning as I tremble under the avalanche of pleasure. I'm barely able to see straight as I collapse. Finn's arm is the only thing holding me up.

As he buries himself to the hilt inside me, I feel the surge of warmth. I'd missed the sensation of coming while being come into *so much.*

In this moment, I forget about everything except him. Oxygen could cease to exist and I wouldn't care because I wouldn't know that death was something that occurred. There's only the two of us.

"I love you," he says.

"I love you," I say, but it's not an echo. I deeply mean every word. He wraps his arms around me, pulling me back to his chest. I enjoy the warmth of his skin, the pressure of his arms around me. They say perfection doesn't exist, but this is perfection. I can't imagine being any happier than I am in this moment, but I am certain there are a million moments that will be nearly as good as long as I'm with Finn.

As hard as I try to stay awake and preserve this moment, my eyelids grow heavy and I fall asleep.

Chapter 18
THE WAIT OF IT ALL

I wake before Finn and want to make breakfast. I'm surprised by this but jump on it while I'm feeling it.

Finn's kitchen is easy to navigate as things are most often in the first place I look. As I organize our classic breakfast of eggs, toast, and jelly onto plates, I begin to feel nervousness in my stomach. It spreads to my arms and even to my face. It quickly graduates to fear.

Being with Finn insulated me from it all. I'd forgotten about Steve, the video, the company, and what ominously towered over my and Finn's life.

He hasn't seemed worried at all so maybe he's been protected by our bubble as well. I want to let him hold onto as much peace as possible before he remembers so I push back the tears and as I hear his steps coming down the hall I call out, "I made breakfast!"

Finn rounds the corner into the kitchen toward a small table that sits in front of a window and looks perfect for breakfast. He is wearing boxers, a tee-shirt, and a huge smile. He looks over the table as I place the final items down. "This looks wonderful, baby girl."

He kisses me on the forehead and we both sit. I pour coffee into his cup as steam rises in front of his face. He hasn't shaved yet so his usual scruff is thicker. I enjoy the distraction this slightly-more rugged look offers, but I still feel the storm in my gut.

As I spoon eggs onto Finn's plate, I feel sick looking at the food. I spoon half as much onto my plate and begin to force myself to eat it with an equally-forced smile. Finn smiles, too, but I notice his eyes slowly go to a spot in the room more than once as he takes a couple of bites.

He lifts his coffee and sips at it, gauging the heat. "Today I'm taking you to—" I'm sure this is the first time I haven't paid attention to his every word. Instead, my attention locks on his eyes as they, once again, casually glance at a spot in the room. I wait until his gaze is back on me for a few seconds so that it won't be obvious that I'm trying to find what he's been looking at. I stand as though I'm going to get something and search the area where he's been looking. I instantly see his phone on the counter.

He hasn't forgotten at all. He's only been protecting me by acting as if nothing were wrong. As if controlled by some other force, I am unable to fight the emotion and break down.

Finn stands, "Baby girl, what's wrong? If it's the food, I'm enjoying it. It's delicious."

He holds me as I cry into his shoulder, his arms swallowing me up and I instantly feel better for a couple of seconds. Then I try to speak. "It's not that. I'm glad you like it, but it's…it's…" I can only speak in a controlled whisper to communicate at all. "Steve is going to take the video to…to—"

"Hush now baby girl. I can't stand to see you this way. It's not worth it."

"Please don't pretend for me. I know what this job means to you. I know it pays a fortune and I know you've worked hard to get here and—"

I'm interrupted, but not by Finn. As he holds me, the only sound being made now is the vibrating pulses of a phone. I can tell by the pulses that it's not my phone—it's Finn's—and something about it tells me exactly what it is. Maybe I was having a bad dream before I woke up, though I don't remember dreaming at all. Maybe it's because I know that if Finn takes an off day that no one is to contact him unless it's an emergency. Maybe I just know that happiness will always be trampled by viciousness.

Finn lifts his chin from resting atop my head and I lower my hands from his chest. His arms unenthusiastically drop from the small of my back and he turns toward the phone. I watch as he looks toward it without leaving his position. The phone call ends before he can answer it, but he doesn't seem fazed.

I walk to the phone and glance at its face. "Who's Jonathan Rust?"

He takes a few steps, toward me before he answers. "One of the board members," he mutters, his lips moving to my shoulder and kissing me through the cotton of my undershirt before continuing. "One of the more nervous ones. He'll call back in a minute."

"What do you think it's about?"

He shrugs. "No idea. Must be important."

"Finn," I say. "Come on. It could be—"

"I'm certain it is," he says as though it's only as troubling as his favorite football team failing to complete a pass with a thirty-point lead.

His phone begins to ring again and we both turn back toward it. He steps away from me as he answers it. "Hey, John. What's going on?"

I check the screen on his refrigerator, desperate for a distraction. There's a lot of fruits, vegetables, bottles of water, various liquors—and a whole ham. I saw all of this earlier, but I don't want to try to decipher his phone conversation in order to figure out if I've officially ruined his life. What else was I expecting? It occurs to me again that Finn had made sure I wasn't thinking about it last night. Too much happiness had existed in being with him again for me to remember the height of the stakes. He didn't want me to worry.

"Just spit it out, John," Finn says. "Say what you

need to say. I won't shoot the messenger…John, I know you're the messenger because they always make you the messenger. That's something you have to take up with them. Just get it over with."

I watch Finn's eyes shift back and forth as he listens. I can't imagine what is going through his mind as everything he has worked for is being taken away from him when he did nothing wrong.

"Okay," he says after a minute or an hour has passed. Time has become inconsequential. "I understand. Thank you."

He puts his phone down on the counter. When he looks at me, I expect him to be angry or upset, but his face is unreadable.

"Finn?"

"The board wants to talk to me today, but it's just a formality," he says. "Steve talked to them and threatened to go to the media."

"Do you think he gave them the recording?"

"There's no reason he wouldn't. I expected him to do no less."

"Maybe you can convince them that I was a crazy stalker or something and that Steve is just as crazy. The second part is true. I'll play along."

He shakes his head. "After you left, there's been a hostile takeover occurring at Torv. A couple of board members had already been floating the idea of bringing in another CEO—Jared Wright's son. There just wasn't a reason before and his experience is questionable. But Jared has a lot of influence over the board."

I pull my arms tight around my waist. "But Torv was profiting more than ever under you."

"That's the only reason I've kept my position since Jared's son left his previous job. But even with his lack of experience, he makes a safer choice in the eyes of the public for them than me with a scandal concerning sexual harassment—"

"I wasn't harassed."

"—a scandal concerning sexual power dynamics, as they'll claim, then, they'll say they don't have a choice. If sex is involved, someone, somewhere will be outraged. And with you being younger...people make up rules on that as well and it seems to having nothing to do with whether or not two people love each other."

"Finn, I don't know what to say. I'm so sorry. There has to be something I can do. I could convince them that the recording was just the ranting of a crazy woman who fantasized that she was sleeping with her boss. That's probably a common thing. They can't blame you for that."

"Sarah." He wraps his arms around me. I loosen my arms from my waist so that I can feel him closer to me. "Before, I was apprehensive at the thought of losing my job and I let that jerk keep his grasp of you. Now, since I brought you here last night, I realize how ridiculous that was. Nothing matters to me if I don't have you. So, what's going to happen is that I will walk into that meeting and I will resign before they can fire me."

"What? You can't do that. No. You don't even know if they're going to fire you yet. It's not fair!"

"It doesn't matter. I've thought about this scenario since we met at that coffee shop. I have no problem with this decision."

"But what else are you going to do?"

"I'm going to start my own business," he says, a smile forming and his eyes dancing with a sudden excitement. "I'll be owner and CEO. I'm thinking Nashville."

He kisses me and he tastes like warmth and sincerity. I kiss him back, all the broken things in me melding and the scars fading away to something smoother and stronger. "Of course, when I start my business," he continues, "I'll need an assistant."

I can't help but laugh, the whole moment feeling extremely genuine and surreal. When we kiss again, it seals a contract between us—a contract I know I could never get out of and I'd never want to. This part of our lives might go out with a bang, but the best things in my life are often accompanied by a fierce blow.

About Tina Sumley

 *Tina Sumley* is an author who writes adult novels that quicken your pulse and excite your senses!

She most often writes about powerful men and the women who love them. She believes that alpha males make life an adventure and writes for women who agree. She also believes in beautiful, passionate love rather than cheap, nameless sex.

If you enjoy reading about the human sexual experience as it ties in with the heart and mind, you'll want to spread open the pages of her books (or at least use your phone or tablet to read them).

Tina prides herself in writing bubble-bath worthy stories. If you're a woman who insists on taking a little time for herself every now and then, you understand exactly what she means.

Visit **TinaSumley.com** for more titles by Tina.

www.ingramcontent.com/pod-product-compliance
Lightning Source LLC
Chambersburg PA
CBHW032209190626
46810CB00019B/2418